RED BLITZ

A thriller

BY JAMES RAVEN

*

Published through
Global House Publishing

Dedicated to Lyanne, Ellie and Jodie
– my three wonderful daughters

James Raven is a former journalist and TV news executive.
His other books include:

Rollover
Urban Myth
After the Execution
Stark Warning
Arctic Blood
Brutal Revenge

http://www.james-raven.com/

Chapter One

The two men walked silently to the very edge of the little landing stage jutting out into the restless waters of the lagoon. They both wore dark sweaters, jeans and leather jackets.

Behind them, the street lights of Venice flickered like precious gems, flushing the majestic façade of the Doges Palace with a soft, warm glow.

When they reached the end of the landing stage the men stopped and listened. The only sound was the slopping of water against the timber piles beneath them. Out across St Mark's basin several lamps burned on the tiny island of San Giorgio Maggiore and away to the right a dozen or so gondolas, moored side by side along the quay, bobbed up and down on the choppy spring swell.

The taller of the two men carried a small canvas bag in one hand. When he was satisfied they were not being observed he put it down beside him. His companion took a flashlight from his pocket. He made sure he was screened from the promenade by the little ferry service waiting room on the landing stage before switching it on. At once both men cast fluid shadows that danced across the timber decking.

The tall man, who stood six three, was in his early thirties, thin-faced and with closely-set eyes sunk deep beneath bushy brows. His hair was thick and dark and curled slightly around the ears.

The other man, slightly older, sported a wider frame, pigeon chest, and short cropped hair. He walked with a barely perceptible limp.

The tall man lowered himself to a squat, unzipped the bag and reached inside. He took from it a saucer-shaped limpet mine measuring fifteen inches in diameter and four inches deep. On one side was a magnetic plate, on the other a small built-in clock-face with setting switch.

The man passed it to his companion who took great care not to drop it. Merely touching the object brought sweat to the older man's forehead and caused his hands to tremble slightly. He’d been told that there was no risk of it going off unexpectedly. All the same he was taking no chances. Any kind of explosive device made him nervous.

The tall man stepped up to the edge of the landing stage and lowered himself down a wooden ladder until he could reach the underside of the decking.

It was criss-crossed by metal beams which at high tide were submerged under several inches of water. His partner delicately passed him the mine and with great care he placed its magnetic side against a horizontal beam. It stuck firmly with a metallic clunk. He flicked on the pre-set timing switch, then grunted his satisfaction and climbed back up the ladder.

"Now we’re ready," he said to his companion. The flashlight was switched off and put away and the tall man bent down to pick up the bag.

It was then he heard the sound of heavy footsteps on the landing stage and froze. The older man instinctively stepped back into the shadow of the waiting room before the unwelcome visitor was upon them.

A uniformed figure appeared from behind the waiting room, and suddenly the tall man was blinded by a fierce light.

"I'm an officer of the Carabinieri," a voice bellowed. "Who are you and why are you here?"

The older man chose that moment to spring out of the shadows and smash a fist into the jaw of the paramilitary cop, who was taken completely by surprise. He dropped his flashlight and staggered backwards, just managing to stop himself falling into the water. But before he could regain his equilibrium the two men were on him.

The tall one kicked him in the left shin while his partner followed through with a blow to the stomach. The cop doubled over and a rush of air escaped from his lungs.

The two men continued to rain blows even after the Carabinieri officer went down and curled his body like a hedgehog. He was kicked in the head, the face and the ribs until he was no longer moaning or moving.

"Is he dead?" the older man said between gasps.

His companion shrugged. "I think so, but let's put him over the side to be sure. He'll drown in minutes."

They lifted the officer's arms and legs and carried him to the edge of the landing stage. Then they dropped him unceremoniously into the water with a heavy splash.

They watched in silence as the dark uniform drifted away from them into the night. Within seconds it had disappeared.

Far out in the lagoon at that moment a ship's hooter sounded, making both men jump.

“We need to get going,” the tall one said, his voice low and urgent.

He picked up the empty bag and they hurried back along the landing stage onto the promenade.

Then they started walking briskly into the city centre.

Chapter Two

The tall man, whose name was Mario Scalise, was among the most wanted terrorists in Italy. He'd been behind many of the anti-capitalist attacks launched by the New Red Brigades in recent years.

He was one of the more fanatical members of the re-invented guerrilla organisation. He was also an acknowledged expert on explosives, which was why he'd been chosen for this particular operation.

On this night he was teamed up with Enrico Barone. Although not so well respected within the movement, Barone was another who was totally committed to the concept of bringing about a revolution in Italy. He was one of the many young tearaways who had turned to terrorism because he saw it as a way out of the economic chaos that was destroying his country.

The two men made their way through the deserted streets of Venice, confident in the knowledge that at this hour there would be few people about.

Venice is a quiet city late at night and even at the height of the tourist season it's nowhere near as raucous as Rome or Milan. Sometimes it appears as though there's a curfew in place. Cats and rats are the only creatures on the prowl and the eerie silence can be claustrophobic.

The two men walked with a spring in their step. They were pleased with themselves. Apart from the problem with the Carabinieri officer, which they felt they had handled with commendable efficiency, everything had gone to plan.

They could only hope and pray that the other teams had been as successful.

Their destination was an apartment in the Cannaregio district, better known as the Jewish quarter of the city, where a ghetto was established in 1516 under the Venetian Republic. The ghosts of persecuted Jews are said to haunt the alleyways and dilapidated buildings. Among them the hundreds of unfortunate souls who were shipped off to the concentration camps during the Nazi occupation of the city in World War Two.

The apartment block was close to the *Museo Ebraico*, the Jewish Museum. It was an imposing building which backed on to a narrow canal. The two men used a security buzzer at the entrance to announce themselves. Once inside they hurried up a winding staircase.

They stopped outside a door on the second landing and Scalise rapped on it with his knuckles, gently so as not to disturb the occupants of the apartment next door.

The door creaked open and a man's face peered out through a gap that was the size of a chain lock. His eyes took in both men quickly, then glanced beyond them to satisfy himself that there was no one else. The door was closed and opened again after the chain had been removed.

The two shuffled into a dimly lit room that consisted of a couple of armchairs, a glass coffee table and a television mounted on a stand. There was a threadbare carpet and a large window with net curtains.

The young man who had opened the door now closed it behind them. He had shaggy brown hair and a round, doughy face. His eyes were dull and sunken and he had an athletic build. He was wearing a black leather bomber jacket, cords and a pair of muddied loafers.

"Mission accomplished, Nicolas," Scalise said.

The young man nodded. "Were there any problems?"

Scalise hesitated. "Just one, but we sorted it."

The young man frowned. "Tell me."

Scalise cleared his throat. "We had to kill a Carabinieri officer on patrol. He came across us while we were working on the landing stage on the Riva Degli Schiavoni."

Nicolas Marsella was not one to show emotion. Whether it be anger or grief or pleasure, he was usually adept at concealing it behind a blank expression. But he responded uncharacteristically to this piece of news. His face clouded and his grey eyes widened accusingly, the black pupils dilating like those of a wary cat.

"Are you out of your fucking minds?" he said. "You might have jeopardised the entire operation."

Scalise merely shrugged, not one to be intimidated by angry outbursts from his superiors.

"We had no choice," he said. "He appeared out of nowhere and took us by surprise."

“Are you sure that you killed him?”

Scalise nodded. “Absolutely.”

"And what of the body?"

"We dropped it into the lagoon."

"So there'll be an investigation. Questions will be asked."

"And unless they've got someone over at the Questura who can communicate with the dead, there's no way they'll find out what the hell happened," Scalise said.

Marsella drew in a ragged breath and walked over to the window. He pulled back the tattered curtain and peered out. The glow of a single street lamp danced on the surface of the canal. It was the only movement out there.

"We were not followed," Barone said as he dropped into one of the armchairs.

Marsella continued to stare out of the window, his body tense, as though ready to strike. Scalise and Barone watched him, waiting and hoping for a pat on the back for a job well done.

As one of the founders of the new movement, Marsella had their respect. His father had been one of the radical students who had given birth to the original Red Brigades back in 1970. The avowed aim of those young anarchists had been to ignite a coup that would force the Italian communists to return to a revolutionary role and spark a civil war that the Left would win.

Marsella senior had been one of the hard core of militants who from the outset had urged that violence should be the backbone of their struggle. And during the Seventies the Brigades ran a campaign of brutal assassinations and kidnappings that placed them among the ranks of the most feared guerrilla groups in the world.

Marsella senior died of a heart attack in 1978 and soon after that the Red Brigades fell apart after a series of mass arrests.

But growing public anger against austerity during Italy's financial crisis, allied with acute mistrust of the scandal-plagued mainstream political parties, had encouraged a new generation of radicals to take up arms.

Radicals like Nicolas Marsella.

At last he turned away from the window and a smile slowly uncoiled on his face.

"So who's for a drink?" he said.

"I thought you'd never ask," Barone replied, relieved.

Marsella went into the kitchen. A bottle of whisky was standing on the worktop, three glasses beside it.

Marsella carried them into the other room. He handed out the glasses and filled each one to the brim.

“I want you both to know that I think you did a fine job," he said.

"I'm just glad that part of the operation is over," Scalise said.

“The other three squads reported in half an hour ago." Marsella told them, raising his glass. "So let us now toast the success of the operation so far."

They all raised their glasses and each of them swallowed about half a measure in one go. As they drank, Marsella strolled around the room. He worked his way behind the armchair in which Barone sat and finished off his drink.

Barone looked up and said, "By the way, who was the fall guy you eventually decided on? I don't think you've mentioned the name of the unlucky bastard. Last I heard you were still trying to come up with someone suitable. You wanted a guy who was known or suspected to be one of us, but he also had to be expendable. I'm curious to know who you picked."

Marsella casually stepped up behind the armchair and put his glass on the sideboard. His right hand went to his pocket and from it he produced a syringe containing a clear liquid. He glanced at Scalise who gave a slight nod and placed his empty glass on the table.

"Well?" Barone said. "Who did you pick? Do I know him?"

Marsella suddenly bent forward and trapped Barone's neck in the crook of his left arm.

Barone's eyes widened in horror and his initial reaction was to try to scream, but Marsella's arm tightened on his throat and cut off any sound.

Barone tried to tear the arm away, clawing at the sleeve, but then Scalise was on him, pinning his arms back and forcing his knee down heavily between Barone's legs.

Marsella raised the syringe and stabbed Barone in the neck. The needle penetrated the flesh about half an inch. Barone struggled briefly and then was suddenly still, as if all his energy was spent.

Marsella unhooked his arm and stood back, panting heavily, the empty syringe in his hand.

Scalise also stood back, letting go of Barone's arms which fell limply into his lap.

Barone stared ahead, eyes glazed, his breathing hoarse, and it was almost as if he was slowly falling into a trance.

"The drug is a digitalis compound," Marsella said after a moment. "A substance that can both stimulate and simulate a heart attack. The dosage I have given you will kill you in less than a minute."

Barone raised his eyes and looked pleadingly at Scalise. He tried to open his mouth, to form words, but the effort was too great. His face was numb and he could feel a tightening sensation across his chest.

"It's no good," Marsella said. "The drug has already begun to work. I know what you are trying to say. You are trying to say why? Why me? Of course, the only answer I can give to you is that we had to sacrifice somebody and since you are known by the authorities to have a heart condition you were naturally the prime candidate."

Barone managed to shake his head and tears welled up in his eyes.

"But you will not be forgotten, Enrico," Marsella went on. "You are dying for the good of the cause and will be remembered as a hero. Your family will be provided for and I hope you will rest content in the knowledge that the success of this most important operation is dependent upon one of us being sacrificed."

Barone began to choke and with each retching movement his pupils dilated. Within seconds his whole body was shaking violently with every heart palpitation. Saliva dribbled from both corners of his mouth onto his chin and his nose began to run.

"Goodbye my friend," Marsella said. "And please, go with the understanding that this was necessary."

Barone gagged one more time, then fell back against the chair, his eyes wide, staring fixedly at the ceiling, his body stiff.

Scalise leaned over and felt for a pulse. "He's dead," he pronounced after a moment.

Marsella returned to the kitchen. He went to a drawer and took from it several sheets of paper with handwriting on them. These he spread about the table top in the centre of the room. He also took from the drawer the pen with which they'd been written. He carried this back into the main room, holding it by the tip, and pressed the index finger and thumb of Barone's right hand against the shaft. He then returned to the kitchen and placed the pen on the table.

Scalise came into the kitchen. "Are you ready?"

Marsella nodded.

They returned to the main room and Marsella slipped the glasses he and Scalise had used into his pockets. He wiped his prints from the whisky bottle and from everything else he had touched.

Then together they carried Barone to the front door. Scalise opened it and looked out into the hall. It was deserted. Leaving the door open, he took hold of Barone's feet and dragged him across the threshold and left him lying in the doorway.

"That will do." Marsella said. "The neighbours can't fail to see him there."

Their work done, they hurried down the stairs, and out into the night. There was nobody about. They turned right and walked parallel with the canal for about a hundred yards. Then they crossed over a small bridge and hurried through an alley to a small, poorly-lit square. Most of the buildings around it were rundown, their stucco facades in desperate need of renovation.

The one they entered was clearly the oldest and most neglected. The front door opened on squeaky hinges and the floorboards in the hallway groaned under their weight.

They dashed up the stairs to the second floor. Marsella knocked on a door that was opened immediately and they were ushered into the apartment by a short man with a beard who led them into the living room where they were greeted by twelve other men, each of whom looked tired and tense.

"It's done, Marsella announced, with a broad grin.

"The poor fuck," someone said. "God rest his soul."

Chapter Three

The first shaft of morning sunlight managed to squeeze into the room through a gap in the shutters. It crawled across the parquet flooring, up onto the bed and across the faces of the two people lying side by side.

Armond Cali felt it stroke his eyelids, a warm, pleasant sensation that had no bearing on his dream. He squinted involuntarily and turned his head to one side, away from the window. But his left eye remained in the light and its warmth and strength soon became an irritation, something his mind could not ignore, and eventually he was awake.

He lay there with his eyes tightly closed, listening to his wife's heavy breathing and thinking that he really ought to get more sleep. Now that the holiday season was virtually upon them and millions of tourists began to converge on Venice, it was only sensible that he should go to bed earlier in the evening. Last night he hadn't turned in much before midnight and now he felt shattered. He knew it was ungraciously early because of the position of the sun and he also knew that he wouldn't be able to go back to sleep now that he was awake.

He yawned, and turned on his side, forcing his gummy eyes open. He studied his wife's profile, set against the hazy glow of morning, and it occurred to him, not for the first time, that she was starting to show her age.

Although her skin was delicately translucent, as it was during her younger years, it was beginning to crease in places and that thick black hair had lost its glossy appearance.

But to him she still possessed the finest qualities of womanhood. Even with all that excess flesh she was still brimming with sexuality, still capable of turning him on like no other woman had ever been able to.

He still loved her, of course, always would, and he was as sure as anyone can be that she still loved him.

A sound beyond the door brought him out of his reverie. One of the boys most likely.

He smiled to himself contentedly. They were great kids. The pair of them. At fourteen Riccardo was the eldest and Cali could see in him the boy he himself was thirty years ago. A street urchin by nature, he was rarely without a collection of cuts and bruises and not a day seemed to pass when he did not return home with his clothes looking as though they had been rinsed out in one of the canals. He was extremely good looking, and Cali didn't doubt that he would have no trouble attracting girls.

Paolo, his other son, was just eleven and already it was evident that he had been cast in a different mould from his brother. He was the studious type, always with a book in his hand and his thirst for knowledge was unquenchable. He had also made it known that he intended to follow in his father's footsteps and become the man in command of Venice's paramilitary police force, the Carabinieri. But Cali preferred to picture Paolo in a lawyer's robes or a surgeon's gown, living in a plush apartment in Rome of Milan. A career in the Carabinieri was not what it once was. The money was poor and the sleek uniform and gleaming boots no longer commanded as much respect.

"Armond darling," Susanna purred suddenly as she turned to face him, her eyes open. “You are awake."

"The light," he said. "It's time I did something about those shutters."

She grinned. "You've said that nearly every morning for the past sixteen years."

"I know, I know. You don't have to remind me of my own failings."

He leaned over and kissed her forehead. Her skin was soft and warm and she smelled of sleep.

"And what was that for?" she asked.

"A gesture of affection my dear. To show you how much I love you."

"Oh really?" she replied with mock suspicion. "I don't suppose you were hoping it would prompt me to return the gesture by offering to get up and make breakfast."

He feigned a hurt look. "Can't I even kiss my wife without being accused of having some ulterior motive?"

"In a word — no."

They both laughed and she nuzzled her head against his chest. He stroked her tangled hair and felt a rush of contentment.

"You're the most devious of men, Armond Cali," she said. "It sometimes puzzles me why I ever married you."

"For my looks?"

She raised herself on one elbow and coolly appraised him. "I think not," she said. "You're not the most impressive of men. What with that receding hairline, those enormous bags under your eyes and that rubber tyre stomach."

"Thanks," he said. "It's nice to wake up to a compliment."

At that moment there was a light tapping at the door. It wasn't unexpected. It happened most mornings.

"Come in," Cali called.

It was Paolo, looking wide-eyed and alert, his hair askew. He walked up to the bed on his mother's side. He was wearing his baggy Spiderman pyjamas.

"It's warm and it's sunny," he said. "Does that mean we can go to the beach?"

Today was Sunday and Cali had promised to take them to the Lido for the day. At this time of the year the beaches were not crowded and the sea could be pleasantly warm. It was only a short way across the lagoon and they went there as a family whenever they could. But it wasn't often because Cali's job was so demanding he rarely got time off.

"Of course," he said to his son. "We'll leave after breakfast."

The boy broke out in a big toothy smile, then turned sharp on his heels and was out of the room in a flash.

"If your office calls I want you to tell them that under no circumstances can you go in today," Susanna said. "For once let them try to run this city without you."

He placed an arm around her shoulders and pulled her towards him. "On one condition," he said.

"What's that?"

"I get two rolls instead of one for breakfast."

"What about your diet?"

"To hell with that. This is my day off. I'll get back to starving myself tomorrow."

*

They were seated around the breakfast table when the phone rang.

"Oh, no," Susanna exclaimed. "I knew it."

"Don't panic," Cali told her. "It could be anyone."

"It's the office. Don't ask me how I know. I just do."

Cali crossed the room to pick up the phone. "Yes?"

"Colonel? It's Salvatore. I'm sorry to trouble you at home on your day off, but I felt it was necessary."

Salvatore Vitale was one of the most highly rated men on Cali's staff. He was diligent and competent and had an assured and good-natured demeanour.

"Go ahead, Salvatore," Cali said with a sigh. "What has happened that is so important you cannot handle it without me?"

"I'd rather not go into details over the phone," Salvatore said. "But it has to do with something our officers found when they were called to a sudden death at a flat in the Cannaregio district. It's something I think you should see."

Cali turned and saw his wife glaring at him through the half open door.

"Can't you be a little more specific?" he said into the phone. "I want to be sure that it's absolutely essential that I should come in before I cancel arrangements that have already been made."

"I don't want to talk about it over an open line, sir," Salvatore said. "But believe me something serious has occurred and it requires your immediate attention."

Cali furrowed his brow. Salvatore wasn't one to exaggerate so if he said something was important – or serious – then it usually was.

"Very well," Cali said. "Send a boat for me."

"It's on its way, Colonel."

Cali hung up the phone with a heavy sigh. He felt a knot of tension in his back as he walked into the kitchen.

"Well?" Susanna said.

Cali shrugged. "Something important has come up."

She shook her head. "I knew this would happen. I just knew it."

"Does this mean we can't go to the beach?" Paolo said, suddenly near to tears.

"I'm afraid so." Cali said.

"But you promised."

"I know and I'm sorry, but it can't be helped. Perhaps we can do something later in the day if I'm not kept away too long."

"I've heard that one before," Susanna chipped in.

Cali shrugged again. "I'm sorry."

He turned away before anything more could be said and walked briskly to the bedroom, the air about him suddenly warm and stuffy. He decided not to wear his uniform. Instead, he put on a suit and strapped his service revolver, a Beretta 92, beneath his jacket. Finally, he picked up his wallet and ID card and slipped them into his pocket.

The bedroom door opened and Susanna came in.

"The boys are terribly upset," she said. "Could you not delegate responsibility just this once?"

"Normally I would," he said. "But this thing, whatever it is, seems to be causing a stir. Salvatore isn't even prepared to give me the details over the phone. He says it's important and requires my attention."

"It always requires your attention, Armond."

He crossed the room to her and put his hands on her shoulders.

"We both knew when I accepted the promotion that it would be a huge commitment to the city and its people," he said. "I have no choice but to respond when there's an emergency. Surely you can see that."

She inhaled slowly and deeply and gave a slight nod.

"It's still not an easy thing to live with," she said.

He squeezed her shoulders. “I know, but live with it we must.”

At that moment the doorbell rang. Cali walked to the window, pushed open the shutters, and looked down. A police launch was below, its engine running.

"I have to go. If I'm back soon we'll go out. I promise."

Susanna shrugged. "I shouldn't hurry if I were you. By that time the boys will be out and it'll take us the rest of the day to round them up again."

He couldn't think of anything more to say so he kissed her gently on the cheek and left the room.

Chapter Four

It was a bright day and warming up by the second. Cali stood at the back of the launch and felt the sun on his face as the pilot negotiated a maze of narrow canals.

Old buildings loomed high and proud on either side, many of them in such poor condition that it was a miracle they were still standing.

As always Cali reflected on the sad fact that his beloved city was doomed. Slowly but inexorably it was sinking into the lagoon. Everyone knew that Venice was living on borrowed time. The grand palaces and churches had been built on ancient wooden pilings sunk into the salt marsh.

For centuries the merciless waters of the Adriatic had been gnawing at those pilings and now, whenever there was an unusually high tide, Venetians put their faith in prayer and asked that their city be spared.

Since 1966, the year of the Great Flood, Cali had shared their concern that things were getting worse. Extreme high tides known as *acqua alta* were becoming more frequent. This was when the water level rose almost four inches above normal, causing extensive flooding, especially around St Mark's

Square. It wasn't unknown for large areas of the city to be evacuated when this happened.

The flood menace was one thing, but the city was also dying of old age. There was evidence of it all around him. Towers that leaned precariously, palaces, once so rich and splendid, crumbling because they were neglected, and paving stones that were out of alignment and quite hazardous.

Venice had always been a city under siege, but at no time in its history had it faced such a tough battle to survive. Even the Venetians themselves were giving into despair and flocking to the mainland in droves. Cali's own brother, Michael, had done just that last year, relocating his family to Trieste after their home was flooded for the umpteenth time.

Cali could not imagine ever following in his brother's footsteps, though. He loved this city too much to desert it. But he had to concede that eventually he might have to.

The police launch entered the Cannaregio district, which on this Sunday morning seemed unusually quiet.

It was one of Cali's favourite parts of Venice, a place rich in history that had remained unchanged for centuries. He knew every synagogue, kosher restaurant and Holocaust memorial. He knew many of the residents too, which wasn't difficult since there were now fewer than fifty of them.

The launch came to a stop next to a small square and Salvatore was waiting on the quayside, resplendent in the blue uniform of the Carabinieri.

Cali heaved himself out of the launch and said, "This had better be important, Salvatore."

Salvatore Vitale was a short, stout man of forty, four years younger than Cali. His skin was weathered, but not wrinkled, and his thick black hair was peppered with grey. He was a family man, with three children and a wife who was a professional artist.

"We have to go to an apartment block that is only a short walk from here," Salvatore said.

"So what's all this about?" Cali asked.

Salvatore gestured for them to start walking. "The state police were called to the building earlier after a man's body was found," he said. "Soon after they arrived they made a discovery which prompted them to call us."

"Care to tell me what they discovered?"

"I'd rather you saw for yourself, sir. We're almost there."

There are several police forces in Italy, among them the Carabinieri, an autonomous branch of the armed forces, and the *Stato Polizia*, or state police. Their functions often overlap, causing constant rivalry, but the most serious crimes, including terrorism, are dealt with by the Carabinieri. So Cali was at once alert to the possibility that something very bad had happened.

It took them only a few minutes to get to the apartment building, which was old and unimpressive. There were five storeys and the ochre coloured stucco had peeled away from much of the façade to reveal dirty grey bricks beneath.

A couple of uniformed police were standing outside the entrance and they both acknowledged Cali with a quick salute.

"The second floor," Salvatore said once they were inside.

The stairway was dark and damp and smelled of decay. By the time they reached the second floor Cali's forehead was beaded with perspiration.

A Carabinieri officer was on guard outside the flat, holstered revolver at his hip. He stood over the figure of a man lying on the floor. The man was on his back, eyes staring at the ceiling, mouth open. He looked to be in his thirties and had cropped hair and wide shoulders. He also looked very dead. His skin was pale and cold and rigor had stiffened his limps. There were no wounds on the exposed flesh.

"He was found by a neighbour," Salvatore said. "The doctor has already seen him and provisionally diagnosed a heart attack."

Cali frowned. "Natural causes? So why all the fuss?"

"That will become evident when we go inside, sir."

"Really? Then I'm intrigued. Do we know who he is?"

Salvatore shook his head. "He's not known to me and we've found nothing in the flat to identify him."

"Did he live here alone?"

"So it would seem. Apparently the apartment was empty until nine days ago when this man moved in. We've spoken to the landlord who lives on the ground floor. The dead man took a six month lease on the apartment but it turns out that the name he gave was false."

They had to step over the body to enter the apartment. Cali's nostrils flared on contact with the musty smell of an aged and decaying interior. It was a smell that he'd grown accustomed to since it was all over Venice, permeating the air in most of the ancient buildings along the Grand Canal and around the Piazza.

Salvatore led the way to the kitchen where the forensic experts were nosing around, notebooks in hand. He took a pair of latex gloves from his pocket and handed them to his boss. Then he gestured towards several sheets of notepaper that were lying on the table.

"Check those out, sir," he said.

Cali slipped on the gloves, then put on his glasses and picked up one of the sheets. His lungs immediately dragged in a hasty breath as he started reading the words that had been scrawled neatly in black ink.

"This is not a hoax. I repeat. This is not a hoax. Unless my demands are met within twenty-four hours, a series of bombs which have been planted throughout the city will be detonated. Only I know where they are and a complete list of locations will be sent to the..."

The writing ended abruptly and Salvatore pointed to another sheet from the table.

"The writer had several goes," he said.

Cali grabbed another sheet of paper and read from it.

"This is not a hoax. I repeat. This is not a hoax. Unless the following demands are met, forty bombs which have been planted in Venice will be detonated simultaneously between midnight and 3am on April 15. To ensure that you take me

seriously an additional twenty bombs will go off throughout the day on the 14th. The first is due to explode at 0900. The second and third bombs will be detonated by timing device four hours later and the others at irregular intervals thereafter. They have been placed so as to cause the maximum amount of damage and only I know where they are. These include limpet mines and magnetic IEDs which are concealed under water and beneath the foundations of buildings.

"A list of locations will be sent to the police when you've done what I ask. Unless you want to see Venice damaged beyond repair, as well as many lives lost, you will not disappoint me. It is not money I want. My motives are purely political. I demand the release of the eight alleged members of the New Red Brigades who are being held in San Vittore prison on charges of subversion pending trial. These people are to be released immediately and given air passage to a country of their choice. I shall of course expect them to be on their way before I send you the list. There will be no more letters and there is no point looking for the explosives. You haven't time. The longer it takes you to realise you have no choice the more damage will be done to your precious city. I say again. This is not a hoax."

Cali's face was drained of colour. He looked up from the letter and nodded towards the table.

"And the others?"

"Attempts at the same letter," Salvatore said. "The one you hold appears to be the finished product. We can only assume he was planning to send the letter to the police or the media."

"What about this list of locations he mentions?"

"No sign of it," Salvatore said. "We've looked everywhere."

Cali gazed in studied disbelief at the note in his hand. He drew a tremulous breath and a chill travelled up his spine.

"Now you see why I felt it necessary to call you," Salvatore said.

Cali nodded slowly. "This is crazy. If this threat is genuine then Venice is faced with a catastrophe." He glanced at his watch. "Today's the thirteenth. That first bomb is supposedly due to go off in twenty-three hours from now."

He forced down a wave of nausea at the thought. Surely it couldn't be real, he told himself. Sixty bombs, for God's sake. It was inconceivable.

"What do you propose to do, sir?"

Cali pulled out a chair and sat down to think about it. In all his years as a cop he had never been confronted by something like this. He stroked his jaw and felt his temple begin to throb.

"Do you think he's telling the truth?" he asked.

Salvatore shrugged. "I don't know. It does sound far-fetched. I mean, surely one man couldn't plant so many explosive devices."

Cali wasn't so sure. Assuming the guy had somehow obtained dozens of bombs and mines then he might have spent weeks or even months planting them all over the city. And it wouldn't be that difficult. Venice was filled with little nooks and crannies. There were a countless number of hiding places. In deserted buildings, exposed foundations, just beneath the surface of the many canals.

He leaned forward, rested his elbows on his knees, and buried his face in his hands. He could feel a lump forming in the pit of his stomach.

He focused his mind on the letter. It gave no indication of anyone other than the writer being involved. If that were so then the only person who knew where the bombs and mines had been planted was now dead. So there was no one with whom they could negotiate. And no one to reveal the locations of the devices.

Shit.

A total of sixty bombs, the letter said. In a city whose buildings rested precariously on millions of wooden sticks driven into the mud. Venice was already crippled by senility and in no fit state to weather such a calamity.

"Is there anything in the apartment to help us?" he asked, looking up.

"We've found nothing so far," Salvatore said. "There are very few personal belongings. You'd never know someone had been staying here in fact."

Cali stood up and wandered over to the door. As he looked at the body lying on the floor he started to feel a little sick and shaky.

"The doctor thinks he was probably trying to get help," Salvatore said. "That's why he was found in the doorway."

Who the hell was he? Cali wondered. A person whose mind had been bent by misplaced idealism or a sadistic maniac who got his kicks from destroying people and things?

Turning to Salvatore, he said, "We've got to come up with a name. Get a photo and prints off to Milan. He may be on file as a member of the New Red Brigades. When you've done that try to trace all his known associates. And get as many people working on it as you need."

"I've already put the wheels in motion, sir."

"Good. I also want you to arrange a meeting as soon as possible in my office with the mayor and the Questore. They should be a party to any decisions I have to make. Tell them only that someone has planted some bombs and is demanding the release of political prisoners. Nothing more. Meanwhile I want this apartment sealed off and everyone in the block interviewed. You'll probably need more men so you have my permission to call in everyone who is off today."

"Anything else, sir?"

Cali nodded. "Get me a copies of these notes and have them check over the originals in the lab. And I'll want you to be present at the meeting with an up-to-the-minute report for me."

Salvatore hurried out of the room. A second later the police doctor entered. He was a diminutive man named Fabio Fellini, with a shock of white hair and shoulders as thin as a coathanger.

"Are you sure this man died of a heart attack?" Cali asked him without preamble.

The doctor pursed his lips and spoke in a high nasal voice. "I won't know for sure until I've opened him up, but that's what it seems like to me."

"No sign of foul play?"

The doctor shook his head. "Nothing superficial. You can see for yourself that there are no marks on his exposed parts. I've checked underneath his shirt."

Cali stared down at the body and felt the rhythm of his heart change. He wanted to believe that the mystery man was a fantasist who had wanted nothing more than to get some attention. After all, such threats were often made and rarely did anything come of them.

But Cali's instincts screamed at him to take this one seriously. There was something about what the man had written that worried him. The amount of detail for one thing. Plus the fact that he had taken such great care to get the wording just right.

It suggested someone with a clear purpose.

Someone who wasn't a time waster.

Chapter Five

Cali and Salvatore talked to other people living in the block. There were three couples and two single men. None of them could shed any light on what had happened and none of them knew anything about the dead man. He hadn't been living in the apartment long and had kept very much to himself.

Only one of the neighbours – a young man who worked in a local restaurant – had actually talked to Barone, and then only to say good evening when he saw him on the stairs two nights ago.

After an hour Cali and Salvatore left the scene and walked back to the launch. The pilot was told to take them straight back to headquarters.

On the way Cali called his wife and explained that he wouldn't be home until late. She wasn't surprised, but the disappointment was evident in her voice. He said he was sorry and left it at that.

The city was bustling as usual. At this time of year there were thousands of tourists on top of the 60,000 residents of the old city. Plus the thousands of people who commuted from the mainland to work in the hotels, shops and restaurants.

Jesus, Cali thought. How could he make sure that all those lives were not in danger? The simple truth was he couldn't – not if there were indeed a bunch of bombs waiting to go off in the city.

He found it hard to get his head around the scale of the threat, even though he still wasn't convinced he should take it seriously. Venice was a small city on a small island and it was extremely vulnerable because it was so densely populated.

He knew the statistics by heart. The city proper, as opposed to the wider metro area that included parts of the mainland, was 457 square kilometres. There were 416 bridges, over 3,000 alleyways, 177 canals, 127 squares, about 7,000 chimneys, 170 bell towers and nearly 500 souvenir shops.

As Cali rolled the figures around in his mind he felt his heart begin to thud against his breastbone. The city would struggle to withstand the impact of just a few large explosions, let alone up to sixty. It seemed impossible that it could happen. And yet what if it did?

What if that many bombs and mines were waiting to be detonated inside buildings and towers and beneath bridges and canals?

It was a frightening prospect and one that caused his stomach to churn with dread.

*

The Carabinieri station occupied a quaint rust-coloured building close to the church of San Zaccaria. It was quiet inside. Word about the dead man and his warning had not yet become widespread. But it soon would.

Cali's office was on the first floor with a view of a picturesque canal. It contained a large mahogany desk, a sofa, four chairs and a couple of filing cabinets. A small TV sat atop one of them.

On the desk was a framed photograph of Susanna and the boys. It had been taken two years ago during a trip to the island of Murano, famed for its glass-making factories and shops. Cali stared at it for a long moment and felt a cold ache form at the base of his skull.

What the hell was he supposed to tell them? That it was possible the city was about to be blown apart! And if so then the bombs could be just about anywhere.

That was a sure way to cause his wife to panic. And who the hell could blame her? It would be the normal reaction. In fact, Cali was well aware that once the news was out Susanna wouldn't be the only one to panic.

It'd be widespread and uncontrollable. People would be justifiably concerned. Many would probably flee to the mainland. Others would in all likelihood go searching for the hidden explosives, thus putting themselves at risk.

Shit.

Before the mayor and the Questore arrived Cali hoped to have a plan of sorts worked out in his mind. Although it was the mayor's city and the Questore was head of the state police, Cali, as commander of the Carabinieri station, would be ultimately responsible for directing a response to this situation.

He couldn’t treat it as an elaborate bomb hoax, even if it turned out to be just that. The circumstances were such that it had to be regarded as a credible threat to Venice and its people. Therefore the authorities had to act accordingly to safeguard the population. But whatever steps were taken were bound to cause alarm on a huge scale.

Cali was still trying to map out his various options when there was a knock at his office door.

"Come in," he said.

It was officer Mario Polensa, a small round-shouldered man who had been posted to Venice from Turin only three months earlier. He had fair hair and a face dusted with a bit of mild acne.

"What is it, Mario?" Cali said.

"Salvatore asked me to tell you that the meeting has been arranged. The mayor and the Questore will be here in forty-five minutes."

"Good. Are you having trouble contacting those officers who are off today?"

"Not so far. It seems most of them had been planning to stay at home."

"I don't suppose anything has come in yet on the identity of the dead man."

"Not yet, sir. His photograph is being circulated and his prints are being processed. Hopefully it won’t be long before we know who he is.”

“Right. As soon as something comes in I want to be informed. And start making arrangements for a briefing session. I’ll convene it as soon as my meeting with the mayor and the Questore is over.

“Very well, sir. Meanwhile, there is something else that I need to bring to your attention.”

"Does it have anything to do with the bomb threat?"

“I don’t believe so.”

Cali shrugged. "Very well, let's hear it."

Mario nodded and stepped nearer to Cali's desk. "It's one of our men, sir. Officer Rienzi. He was badly beaten up last night during a routine patrol."

"Is he all right?"

"He's in hospital, unable to move or talk and barely alive. It appears his attackers left him for dead. They dumped him in the lagoon. He was fished out in the early hours of this morning after he was spotted by a hotel worker. It seems he was lucky not to have drowned. He’s been badly beaten."

"Is he going to live?"

"The doctors say there’s a fifty-fifty chance. I’ve informed his wife."

"Do we know what happened?"

"Not yet. The alarm was raised when he failed to report in after patrolling the Riva Degli Schiavoni. There are several foreign ships in so he may have come up against some drunken seamen"

"It's a possibility. Where exactly was he found?"

"Up against the steps under the Ponte dell Paglia."

"That's only a few hundred yards from here."

Mario nodded. "It seems likely he was attacked shortly around two this morning."

Cali shook his head and made a mental note to go to the hospital at the first opportunity. At any other time an attack on one of his officers would have sparked a major response. But right now it was not the number one priority.

"Keep me informed of the officer's progress," he said. "But assign only a small team to the case until I tell you otherwise. We may well need every available body on this other thing."

Chapter Six

Both the mayor and the Questore arrived a few minutes before the meeting was due to start. They entered Cali's office together and the looks on their faces told him they had already been put in the picture.

Mayor Calvosso, a grey-haired man in his early sixties, wore an expression that aged him about ten years. He'd held office for the past nine months and in that time had impressed everyone, including Cali. He was that rare thing in Italy – an honest politician, who was committed to the people and not focused on feathering his own nest.

Cali's good friend Angelo Lombardo was the chief of the state police in Venice, or the Questore. He was in his mid-forties, with dark wavy hair and a ruddy complexion. He wore a midnight blue shirt and his sleeves were rolled up to reveal tattoos on his forearms.

Cali and Lombardo shared a good working relationship, despite the rivalry that existed in the lower ranks.

Salvatore entered the room after the others and closed the door behind him. The three men sat down. Without preamble, Cali said, "How much do you know?"

Lombardo shrugged. "Only what Salvatore has told us and that isn't much. He says someone has planted some bombs in the city and is demanding the release of a bunch of prisoners."

Cali nodded gravely. “At this stage we can’t be sure if the threat is genuine, but if it is we have a major problem."

Lombardo and the mayor exchanged anxious glances. "What do you mean?" Lombardo said.

Cali took a deep breath and told them about the dead man and the letter found in the apartment.

He dug into his pocket for a copy of the note. "Seems he never lived long enough to send it,” he said.

He passed the note to the mayor, adding, "We don't even know who he was going to send it to."

The others sat in silence while the mayor read it through. His eyes were wide when he came to the end and as he handed the note to Lombardo, Cali saw that his hands had started to shake.

"And you say this man is dead?” Lombardo said. “When? How?"

"His body was found by neighbours this morning,” Cali said. “He’d collapsed in the doorway of an apartment he was renting in Cannaregio. The doctor believes he had a heart attack."

“Did he live there by himself?” Lombardo asked.

Cali nodded. “So it would seem. And that’s the problem. It makes it difficult for us to verify the authenticity of the letter.”

Lombardo mulled this over and said, "So if it's genuine – and this man was indeed working alone – then what does that mean?"

Cali looked at him, his expression solemn. "It means the only person who can tell us where the bombs and mines are hidden is no longer in a position to do so," he said.

"So what about this list of locations he talks about?" the mayor asked. "Can we not find it?"

Salvatore shook his head. "I've just spoken to the officer in charge at the apartment. They've carried out a thorough search and there's no sign of such a list."

"And the man's identity?" the mayor asked.

"We're still waiting," Cali said. "We should know soon enough if he exists on our files."

"But this is terrible." The mayor's voice was filled with panic. "Is there nothing we can do?"

"That's why I've asked you both here," Cali said. "We have to work out a plan of action and fast."

"Then I suggest we get as many people looking for these bombs as we possibly can," the mayor said. "We have…"

"Now hold on just one minute," Lombardo broke in. "Let us not over-react. We can't even be sure this letter is not a hoax. Surely we shouldn't accept it at face value. We could cause a major panic in the city for no reason. To begin with it seems inconceivable that someone could obtain such a large number of bombs and mines."

"Explosive devices are easy to come by," Cali said. "The arms trade is flourishing across Europe and the Middle East. Terrorists can lay their hands on virtually anything, especially IEDs. Three months ago a lorry was stopped en route to Iraq from Greece. It contained no fewer than fifty limpet mines and a hundred AK forty seven rifles."

The mayor swallowed hard. "OK, so we accept that a terrorist group can lay its hands on up to sixty bombs, but surely a person working alone wouldn't be able to plant them. That's absurd."

"Not necessarily," Cali said. "It would be relatively easy to plant a number of devices over a period of time. A handful a day maybe. Hidden in places with easy access, such as abandoned buildings – of which there are plenty in Venice. They'd have to be on a timer, of course, and have an antenna mechanism for remote detonation."

"For that reason we can't afford to ignore the note," the mayor said. "If we do and it turns out not to be a hoax, then God help us."

"So what do we do?" Lombardo asked. "If we tell everyone that dozens of bombs have been planted in Venice and are about to go off it'll lead to mass hysteria. But we can't just wait around until the first one explodes tomorrow. For all we know it might be under a building that will be packed with people."

Cali knew the letter could not be ignored, but there was a good case for not bringing it to the attention of the public at this early stage.

"I think a search should be mounted," he said. "But it must be discreet and the public should not be made aware of what we're looking for. If we do find even one device we'd be in a position to take further action, perhaps call in the army."

"But there's a crucial time factor in this if the letter is to be believed," the mayor said. "What could we possibly hope to achieve in twenty-two hours by doing what you suggest?"

"Assuming the bombs are there and we do find one, we'd then be in a position to justifiably alert the public to the situation," Cali explained.

At that moment the phone on the desk rang. Cali answered it abruptly and as he listened he felt a flash of alarm. He returned the receiver to its cradle and said, "They've identified the dead man. He was well known to the division of general investigations in Milan. His name was Enrico Barone and until recently he was known to be an active member of the New Red Brigades. It's significant to point out that he spent six months in prison two years ago and while there he had a minor heart attack which he managed to recover from."

Lombardo said, "Did you say he was a member of the New Red Brigades until recently?"

Cali nodded. "Apparently word filtered through to the anti-terrorist squad several months ago that Barone had fallen out of favour with his comrades. It was said he had upset them by opposing their violent methods. They say this latest move of his was possibly an attempt to get back into their good books, which is an indication of course that he was acting alone."

"But surely it wouldn't be that difficult to find at least some of the bombs if there are so many out there," the mayor said.

"If Barone went to all that trouble to plant the devices, then he would have concealed them very well," Salvatore said. "And we must not forget that limpet mines can be hidden under water."

"We should start the search immediately," Cali said. "But we'll try to keep it low key. If all our forces work together we should be able to cover the city fairly thoroughly between now and tomorrow morning."

"And if we do find a bomb?" the mayor asked.

Cali thought for a moment, then said, "I suggest we seriously consider bringing in the army to help us evacuate the entire city."

Lombardo's jaw dropped. "You can't be serious. The city of Venice has over sixty thousand residents, plus God knows how many tourists and mainland commuters."

"We'd have to make it possible," the mayor said. "We have emergency evacuation plans in the event of serious flooding. We would have to work those up."

"But we've never attempted anything on this scale," Lombardo said.

"Neither had the authorities in New York before they ordered the mandatory evacuation of hundreds of thousands of people in the face of hurricane Sandy," Cali pointed out. "But they pulled it off in no time at all."

"And I'm sure we'd be able to pull it off too," the mayor said. "I strongly suspect we'll be forced to go for it anyway. We have no idea how powerful these bombs are, assuming they exist that is. Whole buildings could be demolished. And if forty of the damned things go off simultaneously then God only knows how many people would be killed."

"First let's start looking," Cali said. "We can continue to discuss the situation during the rest of today and if there are any further developments we can act on them." He turned to Salvatore. "Try to find out where Barone has been these past few weeks and what he's been up to. Find out for certain whether he has any accomplices. I also want you to organise the teams. Tell them only that we're looking for a handful of explosive devices and they could be anywhere in the city. Tell them also that they must keep it to themselves."

"We should concentrate the search on tourist attractions and empty buildings to begin with," Lombardo said.

Cali nodded in agreement. "We also need to coordinate our efforts. We should get the bomb squad on stand by and alert the military."

Cali got to his feet and looked at his watch. "I suggest we meet back here in three hours. I intend to return to the flat to make sure there aren't any clues that have been overlooked."

Cali turned to the mayor. "Mr Mayor, I suggest that you work up the plan for evacuating the city. Obviously there would be the question of transport to consider and also how to relay the information to the public. I'll leave it to your department to come up with some ideas."

"I'll get to work on it immediately," the mayor said.

Cali exhaled a lungful of air and said, "Hopefully when we next meet the situation will be more encouraging."

But his expression betrayed the fact that he didn’t actually believe that.

Chapter Seven

Vittore Greco was a handsome 25-year-old with olive skin and eyes the colour of tarnished brass. His dark hair was cropped and he had the physique of a body builder.

Of the six men in the room he was the youngest. He was also the most nervous. This was because he was the one with most to lose if things did not work out. His pride more than anything else would suffer and to such a man that was as disastrous as losing a limb.

When at last the phone rang, he sat back in his chair and waited while Nicolas Marsella listened to what the caller was saying.

It took only a minute. Then Marsella replaced the receiver. He was smiling when he turned towards the others.

"They're falling for it," he said.

Suddenly Greco's nerves evaporated and a moment later he was laughing along with everyone else.

When the laughter subsided, Marsella said, "Frederico says the Carabinieri colonel Cali has been to the apartment and now there are guards stationed outside. Frederico has also spoken to his contact inside the Questura who has told him that the Questore is at this moment attending a meeting with the colonel and the city mayor. Obviously they're taking the threat seriously. It's my guess they've already identified Barone. Soon they'll know everything about him, including his heart trouble and the stories we've been putting around of late."

Greco was filled with a deep sense of accomplishment. It was the same feeling he had experienced immediately after committing his first act of terrorism.

That was three years ago, in Rome, when he had attached an incendiary device to the underside of a bus in the busy city centre. Four people perished in the flames and he had watched from a nearby park bench, quite unmoved by the screams of the dying passengers who burned alive trying to escape.

He had been drawn to the new guerrilla movement because of his country's economic meltdown. For him the New Red Brigades offered the only hope for the future. The old order had cost lives as well as jobs and it was time to sweep it away.

It had taken him a while to acquire a taste for violence. He was influenced a great deal by the words of one of the original Brigade leaders who had said, "Revolutionary violence is imposed on us by a situation which is structurally violent." Words such as these had a profound effect on Greco in those early days. They helped convince him that terrorist tactics were morally justified in the fight for a better, corrupt-free society.

He was not one of the most influential members of the organisation, but he was the one who had come up with the idea for this operation. An operation that he reckoned would go down in history as one of the most diabolical crimes ever committed.

The seed had begun to geminate a year ago after he visited his grandfather in the hospice where he was seeing out his final days. The old man had decided to unburden himself of a secret he had harboured for decades. A secret he'd decided he didn't want to take to his grave.

Greco had listened intently and had at first found it hard to believe that his grandfather was not making the story up. After all, it was an extraordinary tale and one that would be hard to prove.

Nevertheless, he had set out to do just that.

It took him four months to establish beyond reasonable doubt that what he'd been told was almost certainly true. He'd checked the story out as best he could with libraries and war archives. He'd collected facts from a variety of sources and only when he was satisfied that his grandfather hadn't made the story up did he go to his Brigade supervisors. It wasn't hard to convince them that his plan could work. They had the resources and the audacity to go for it. They also had a stockpile of explosives, built up over several years.

Now, sitting here in this grimy little apartment waiting to see how the authorities would react to the threat that was hanging over the ancient city, he reflected on the success of the operation so far.

Enrico Barone's body had been found along with the note. The authorities were no doubt trying to decide whether to take it seriously or not. But ultimately they would have to.

The bombs and mines were in position and merrily ticking away. The first was timed to go off at nine tomorrow morning. If the authorities hadn't decided before then to begin evacuating the city then they surely would after that first blast, in which a number of people would probably be killed.

Chapter Eight

"It's official," said the mayor. "There's fog on the way. It should reach us by about five."

Cali sank back into his chair and his shoulders sagged despondently. Venice is famous for its soup-like spring and winter fogs which roll in from the sea like gigantic clots of soggy cotton wool, consuming everything in their path, choking the alleys and squares and settling upon the cold, still canals as might thick swirling foam.

They were in Cali's office. Lombardo, the mayor and Salvatore. Outside, the sky was an unblemished blue and Venice was bathed in brilliant sunshine. But inside the atmosphere was taut with tension and despair.

They'd just been told by Salvatore that no bombs or mines had been found. Teams with sniffer dogs had been searching for hours, mainly around those areas that attracted most tourists.

It seemed an impossible task. Even in a city just two miles long by one mile wide there were an incalculable number of places to conceal a bomb.

And of course many parts of Venice were inaccessible except by boat and scores of buildings were uninhabited because of their age and condition. In many ways Venice was its own worst enemy.

And now the fog, which would no doubt hinder, if not halt the search operation during the night.

“What’s the latest on Enrico Barone?" Lombardo asked.

“Not good news,” Cali said. “The anti-terrorist squad say he’s been off the radar for a while.”

“So we can do nothing except sit it out,” Lombardo said. “Even if our men find one or more bombs in the next couple of hours the fog could well prevent us from doing anything more until morning."

"That's about the size of it," Cali said. "I fear it’s going to be a long night."

*

By early evening a cloying fog had descended on large parts of the city. In the Castello district visibility was down to just a couple of yards.

Most of the Dorsoduro district was shrouded too and in the port area it was so thick two large ships were swallowed up. The fog blurred the shapes of buildings and muffled the sounds of the city. It also hindered the search for hidden bombs.

For those in authority who knew what was going on the silence and stillness was oppressive, infuriatingly so.

Cali kept himself busy. He returned to the apartment in the Jewish quarter where Enrico Barone’s body was found, but there had been no significant developments.

The forensic technicians had managed to confirm that the only prints found were those belonging to the dead terrorist.

Cali called his wife at 6:pm to tell her he'd be working late. It came as no surprise to her. She told him the boys were having dinner and had made the most of the day by playing outside with friends.

"So when will you be home?" Susanna asked him.

"I'm not sure," he said. "I'll get something to eat in the staff canteen."

"Are you all right, Armond? You sound strange."

He wanted to tell his wife what was happening but he didn't want to do it over the phone.

"I'm fine," he said, after a hesitant moment. "Just tired."

"So what's going on?" she asked. "It's obviously pretty serious if you can't get away."

"I'll tell you later. And I'm sorry I can't be there."

"I've forgiven you," she said. "But I can't say the same for the boys."

He laughed. "I'll make it up to them. What do you say we get together and plan a holiday?"

"That's a great idea, Armond. As long as we can count on you not to cancel it at the last minute."

Chapter Nine

An operation centre was set up in the Carabinieri headquarters. By 7:pm thirty officers and administration staff were crammed inside, manning phones, co-ordinating the activities of the officers on the street and liaising with all the other law enforcement agencies across Italy and the rest of Europe.

Direct links had been established with the anti-terrorist squad, MI6, the CIA and Interpol. Every effort was being made to find out all there was to know about Enrico Barone. So far they knew the guy was an anarchist who had served time in prison where he was treated for a heart condition. He'd apparently had an irregular heart beat and had been on medication for some time. Prison doctors had confirmed that he had been a prime candidate for a heart attack and the fact that he'd apparently died of one did not surprise them.

All his friends and relatives were being tracked down and a dossier on Enrico Barone would soon be as thick as an encyclopaedia.

There was still no information, however, on Barone's movements in recent weeks. No one knew where he'd been and who he'd spent time with. Or if they did thcy weren't saying.

Despite the fog the search for the bombs continued, although in some areas it wasn't easy.

Teams of officers worked discreetly in and around public buildings. Police launches cruised the canals where officers looked for anything unusual above and below the waterline.

But no devices were discovered and Cali was beginning to wonder if the letter they'd found had been a hoax after all.

At 11:pm he called home. But Susanna didn't answer the phone so he assumed she was asleep. It wasn't unexpected. She usually went to bed around ten and quite often he wasn't home by then. He was glad, of course, because it meant he didn't have to explain why he wasn't lying beside her.

As the night dragged on every muscle in Cali's body ached with a feverish intensity and a wave of exhaustion settled over him. But he remained alert, even as a looming sense of dread hovered in his stomach.

In the morning the sun rose slowly, nudging away the mist and the dead cold darkness.

Lombardo and the mayor stayed awake throughout too and Cali was comforted by their presence in the operation centre. They agreed with his decision not to go public with the threat contained in the letter. Until they could be sure the bombs were out there they decided to hold fire on any evacuation plan.

If panic seized the city for no good reason then a lot of damage could be done, not least to the credibility of the police. Besides, they were all too aware that they had left it too late anyway. It wouldn't be possible to move a significant number of people before 9:am when the first bomb was apparently due to explode.

Chapter Ten

The Basilica of St Mark is the centrepiece of Venice. It stands in all its splendour at one end of the great and colourful Piazza, a monument that represents all the political, religious and social elements of the Republic.

Built in the 11th Century, the city's cathedral encompasses a mixture of styles ranging from Byzantine to Gothic and yet still manages to convey an impression of harmonious beauty. It is without doubt the most striking building in the city, some would say in all Europe, and naturally every visitor makes a point of seeing it. Nicknamed 'the Church of Gold' because of its opulence, it has been the seat of the Patriarch of Venice since 1807.

On this particular morning the groups of sightseers were out early. They were gathered in front of the basilica, admiring its magnificent facade. Some were studying its five elegant entrances that were constructed in the Romanesque style, while others were taking photographs of the beautiful mosaics in the bowl-shaped vaults of the four arches. Many more were simply standing around, chatting or gawping or feeding the pigeons.

Scaffolding had been erected around the arch supports on the end nearest the neighbouring Doges Palace. The scaffolding was being used by workmen who had for some months been cleaning and restoring the precious stonework. Unfortunately all the best buildings had to suffer this indignity. Naturally it detracted from the appearance of the basilica and it wasn't unknown for tourists to complain about it in writing to the council.

As always, however, the sun brought out the best in the basilica despite the scaffolding. It accentuated the colours of the mosaics in the portals and arches, it defined superbly the rich marble decorations of the exterior and it played on the backs of the four bronze horses that watch over the Piazza from their platform above the main entrance.

By 8.49am there were about a hundred people standing within twenty feet of the towering facade, all of them awed by its beauty and oblivious to what was about to happen.

*

In Cali's office the tension was almost unbearable. Like the countdown to a billion dollar spaceflight. With Cali was Lombardo and the mayor.

In the minutes before nine o'clock no one spoke. The ticking of the wall clock was like the monotonous pounding of a drum. Frequently one of those present would realise there were beads of sweat on his forehead and he would try to wipe them away without the others noticing.

Cali was at the window, his eyeballs tingling as he stared out on the little square and across at the magnificent church of San Zaccare. People were milling about, some hurrying to work, others strolling along enjoying the sights.

Cali suddenly felt a deep sense of responsibility for them. He had agonised over his decision not to warn the public of the possible threat to the city. And he was convinced himself that there was no point even now in precipitating a situation in which fear could lead to panic.

But all the same the decision weighed heavily on his mind.

He checked his watch for the umpteenth time. Less the five minutes to nine o'clock. He'd called his wife an hour ago to apologise for not coming home and now he suddenly felt compelled to call again. Susanna was surprised to hear from him and said as much.

"I just wanted to make sure that everything is OK," he said.

"Of course it is," she responded. "Why wouldn't it be? The boys are up now and having breakfast and I've told them to spend the morning cleaning their rooms."

Cali was thankful that the boys were on a school break. He thought they would at least be safe in the apartment if there was an explosion somewhere in the city.

But knowing his family were not out on the streets did not dull the fear that was pulsing in his veins.

"Look, I'm afraid I have to go," he said to Susanna. "I've got to take a call."

“Call me later,” she said. “I’m curious to know what’s going on.”

He hung up and turned back into the room. Lombardo and the mayor were both watching the clock.

The second hand moved beyond the twelve. The hairs on Cali’s neck bristled and his heart rate tripled.

Five seconds ticked by.

Ten.

Twenty.

The mayor was the first to break the silence. "So it was a hoax after all," he said in a voice that was little more than a ragged whisper.

"Well, thank God for that,” Lombardo said.

But at that very moment there was a distant rumble that sent shockwaves through Cali’s body and seemed to shake the very foundations of the city.

*

“Holy fuck,” Lombardo yelled as he leapt to his feet, his whole body shaking like jelly. "Where was it?"

Cali was at the window, staring out, his face suddenly white. In the distance he saw smoke rising above the rooftops. The smoke was spiralling upwards and spreading out to form an ugly black cloud.

Cali cast his eyes down to the street. People were suddenly still, shocked into immobility by the blast and wondering what had caused it.

For about thirty seconds nobody moved in the office. Then Salvatore burst in and announced that the explosion had taken place in St Mark's Square.

Cali felt his heart drop to the floor. His thoughts tossed around in a sea of confusion and a cold sweat made his palms sticky.

"I can't believe it's happened," he said. "I was beginning to think, to hope…"

"We all were," Lombardo said. "But we now know that the bastard meant business."

"God help us if there are another fifty nine of the fuckers," the mayor said, his voice high with hysteria.

"I'll go over there," Salvatore said. "We need to see how much damage has been done."

"We should all go," Cali said and as they headed for the door they heard the manic bursts of sirens across the city.

*

Devastation greeted them when they reached the Piazza. Cali had never seen anything like it. People were running in all directions, utterly confused. Screams of anguish filled the air. He counted at least five bodies sprawled out on the ground in front of the basilica.

One was that of a small boy and leaning over him was an hysterical woman wearing a large saucer-shaped hat and a camera around her neck. The boy, it seemed, had been standing close to the part of the church that was being restored. Enormous strips of scaffolding had crumbled to the ground only a few feet away from him, one thick piece of rusted metal crushing his right arm into a bloody pulp. Beyond the boy was a mountain of mangled metal and masonry and Cali guessed straight away where the bomb had been hidden.

The basilica itself was in a terrible state. Three of its arch supports had been demolished and a section of the famous catwalk had collapsed in a raging cloud of dust and smoke.

The blast had sent bits of the basilica far out into the huge Piazza and into the smaller square known as the Piazzetta which branches off at right angles and runs to the water's edge.

Already teams of Carabinieri and state police were converging on the area and men with stretchers were hurrying through the milling mobs from their floating ambulances.

Cali, along with Lombardo and the mayor, moved forward for a closer look and saw more casualties on the ground.

One was a woman aged about thirty. A shirt-sleeved man was squatting beside her, blood streaming from a deep gash in his right cheek. He was shaking his head and crying uncontrollably and Cali was almost moved to tears himself by the injustice of it.

Behind them a crowd was beginning to form and Carabinieri in flak jackets were trying to keep them back.

Salvatore left Cali's side for a few minutes to speak to some of the officers and civilians. When he returned, he said, "Quite a few people saw it happen. They say the blast came from behind those boards. It just blew the boards out and those people who were standing close by had no chance."

"But didn't our men search this area yesterday?" Cali queried.

"I believe so. Obviously it was well hidden."

"Or our men didn't look hard enough," Cali said sharply.

"They did their best, Colonel."

Cali turned on Salvatore, an angry glint in his eyes. The utter futility of Salvatore's words caused all the fear and apprehension that had festered inside him during the past twenty-three hours to manifest in a burst of fiery hot venom which rose up from his stomach, making his lips quiver and his cheeks burn.

"Then their best is damn well not good enough," he yelled. "They were told to search this particular area thoroughly. Surely those workings should have been considered a likely spot. It's incompetence I tell you and so help me some blockhead is going to have to answer for it."

He continued to stare balefully at Salvatore, his fists clenched, his neck muscles taut as wire cables.

But almost as quickly as it had flared up, Cali's anger subsided and he became suddenly aware of himself. Several people, including two press cameramen, were standing close by, watching him. He immediately regretted his outburst. It was quite uncharacteristic of him.

He turned to Salvatore, who was biting his bottom lip and looking off into the distance.

"I'm sorry, Salvatore," he said, and relief flooded into the officer's frozen features. "It's just that…"

"No need to explain, Colonel," Salvatore said. "We all feel the strain. And you're right. The bomb should have been discovered."

Cali nodded. "Speak to the men. Instil in them the necessity to be thorough. And then get every man we've got out onto the streets. I want this city turned inside out."

Salvatore seemed grateful for the opportunity to excuse himself from the group. When he was gone Cali turned to Lombardo.

"According to Barone's letter we have four hours before two more bombs go off. How do you think we should play it?"

"Maybe there won't be any more explosions," Lombardo said. "He might have planted just the one device, expecting us to fear the worst and release those prisoners."

"Highly unlikely," Cali said. "And we can't take that chance."

Cali looked again at the appalling scene in front of the basilica. Sweat glistened on his forehead and his legs felt heavy. Amid the confusion a semblance of order was slowly being restored. The stretcher-bearers were carrying the injured to the ambulances and the dead had been covered with grey blankets.

Cali's mind flashed back to Barone's letter. The terrorist had claimed that a total of sixty bombs had been planted in the city. Could there really be another fifty-nine out there, hidden below the water, beneath bridges, behind doors, in attics, under the very foundations of the city?

Yesterday he would have said it was impossible. But now he wasn't so sure.

Chapter Eleven

The best view of Venice is from the gallery atop the Campanile, or bell tower, which soars 324ft above the Piazza. The Campanile, built in 1912 to replace the original one which collapsed ten years earlier, stands opposite the basilica and in years past it has been used as a gun turret, weather vane, watch tower and signal beacon.

Now it was being used by three men who wanted to observe from the best possible vantage point the goings-on in the Piazza directly below them.

Marsella, Greco and Scalise were pleased with what they had seen so far. The blast had been more spectacular than they'd expected. They had hoped for two or three dead, but it was clear that there were at least five corpses.

They hadn't expected the bomb to cause so much damage either. But then it wasn't really surprising considering the age of the basilica.

They'd watched it all. The blast itself which tore great chunks of concrete from the front of the building and hurled them all over the Piazza, the falling bodies, the panic, the tears, the noise. Then the sirens and the gathering crowd of ghouls, the mountain of rubble, the stretcher-bearers and the blood and smoke and dust.

It had been a spectacular show.

"There's the Carabinieri Colonel," Scalise said, peering down through binoculars. "I'm sure that's the mayor who's with him. I don't recognise the one on the left."

"Angelo Lombardo?" Greco said. He too was observing the scene through a pair of binos. "The Questore."

"You did a good job with that first device, Mario," Marsella said. "Let's hope that's all it takes to convince them they should evacuate the city."

"And if it doesn't?"

Marsella shrugged. "If this one doesn't the next two will for sure."

*

Cali stood in the Piazza staring at the carnage. A potent cocktail of fear and rage surged through him. His heart was pounding so hard he could feel the blood rush in his ears.

He told himself he wasn't to blame. He couldn't have known for sure that the threat was genuine. Therefore it would not have been right to raise the alarm as soon as they found Barone's body and the note he'd written.

But it didn't help.

The guilt was growing inside him like an unwanted tumour. Five people were dead. At least a dozen more had been injured. And immeasurable damage had been done to the city's most iconic building.

He found it difficult to form a coherent thought. Every muscle in his body felt rigid. He did not want to believe that there were another 59 bombs out there merrily ticking away. But he knew now that he had to assume there were and take appropriate action.

A siren blared and the shouting around him continued. Anger blazed inside him as he watched his officers fighting to contain the chaos.

It was an incongruous sight. Nothing like it had ever happened in Venice. Even during World War Two Venice was left alone by the bombers, unlike other European cities. But now it was at the mercy of a dead terrorist.

The clock was ticking and they had no idea where the next explosion would take place. Had Barone targeted the city's main tourist attractions? Should they concentrate their efforts on buildings that were undergoing repairs or renovation?

The only thing Cali knew for certain was that they needed to double their efforts. More troops would have to be drafted in immediately to help with the search. Every building, street, alleyway and canal had to be regarded as a potential target.

And maybe it was time the people of Venice were told what was going on.

Chapter Twelve

Cali started preparing for a press conference as soon as he arrived back at his office. He had help from Lombardo and the mayor and the department's team of PR executives.

At the same time there were constant interruptions from Salvatore who had been told to keep them updated.

And the news coming in wasn't good. A sixth person had died from his injuries. He was a Japanese tourist who had been standing directly in front of the basilica when the bomb went off.

To make matters worse no other bombs or mines had been found, fuelling speculation that maybe they didn't exist.

So how much should Cali reveal to the media? That was the most difficult issue to address. Tell the people of Venice that their city was littered with enough bombs to blow it apart and that was sure to cause mayhem.

And what fools they would look if they sparked a disastrous evacuation and nothing else happened.

"This is a hell of a position to be in," the mayor said, echoing the thoughts of everyone in the room.

The presser got under way half an hour later. It took place in the large conference room because so many people turned up. There were newspaper reporters and TV crews and they were all desperate for information on the explosion that had shaken Venice.

The police hadn't actually confirmed that it was a terrorist attack, but nobody was in any doubt that it was.

So far there had been no leaks about the discovery of Barone's body and the letter he had written. Cali was pleased about that. It meant he was still in control of the flow of news. But he was pretty certain that that situation wouldn't last.

He was nervous as he stood in front of the lectern. He could feel the blood roaring in his ears. He wasn't used to being in the limelight and he felt uncomfortable. He thought about his wife and two sons and a spasm of fear rumbled in his stomach.

He was becoming increasingly concerned for them. Like everyone else in the city they were not safe and he knew he would never forgive himself if anything happened to them.

He pushed the thought to one side and concentrated on his breathing as the media representatives settled into the seats. He judged there to be about twenty of them and there were many he had never seen before.

Eventually a restless silence prevailed and Cali started to speak, his voice loud and strident as he tried not to let the fear show.

He began by thanking everyone for coming and then confirmed that the explosion at St Mark's Basilica had indeed been a terrorist attack.

"A full investigation is under way and we're already in possession of information which suggests it was the work of a single individual," Cali said.

"As a precautionary measure we've launched an extensive search throughout the city to ensure that no other devices have been planted."

He paused to swallow against the dryness in his throat. He knew that at least one TV station was transmitting the feed live to its viewers and it made him feel self-conscious.

How am I coming across? he wondered. *Do I look nervous? Scared. As though I'm not in control of the situation?*

"I appeal to the public to remain vigilant," he said after a few seconds. "This was a diabolical attack on our great city and I offer my condolences to the families of those who've been killed. A number of people have also been injured and we will make sure they receive the best treatment possible."

Cali paused again and blew out a heavy breath. His face was red and a vein throbbed across his forehead.

The questions started to fly at him before he continued speaking but he was glad of it because he felt he had run out of things to say.

"What evidence do you have that only one person was behind this?" said a journalist who failed to identify himself.

"I'm afraid I can't reveal those details just yet," Cali said. "The investigation is at an early stage and certain information is extremely sensitive."

"But do you know the identity of the terrorist?" the journalist persisted. "Is it a man or woman?"

Cali cleared his throat and felt a bead of sweat trickle down the back of his neck. There was a roar inside his head that seemed louder than a jet engine.

"Look, you have to appreciate that I can't be as forthcoming as I'd like to be," he said. "Not until I can be absolutely sure of all the facts. My first priority is to make you aware of the general situation and inform the public that there might be a risk of further explosions. Beyond that you'll have to be patient with us."

More questions came thick and fast and there was no holding back.

Were the authorities warned it was going to happen?

How many officers are involved in the search for the bombs?

How much damage has been done to the basilica?

Is this the work of the New Red Brigades?

What advice do you have for people who are scared? Should they leave the city?

This last question sent his body temperature rocketing. He rubbed his upper lip with his forefinger and said, "We don't know for certain if there are more bombs. So far we haven't found any and for that reason we feel there's no need for people to panic and rush to the mainland."

His throat tightened as he spoke because he knew that what he had just said would be seized upon.

And it was – by a young woman who said she was a reporter with CNN. Next to her stood a man with a camera.

“But isn’t it true, Colonel, that no one in the city is completely safe at this time?” she said. “After all, if there are any other devices then they could be hidden just about anywhere.”

Cali felt his heart trying to punch its way out of his ribcage. As he responded to the reporter he tried not to stumble over his words.

“It’s true that at this point the whole city is potentially at risk,” he said. “But that’s what happens following a terrorist attack anywhere in the world. It’s impossible to know if in the immediate aftermath there’ll be further attacks.”

The CNN reporter opened her mouth to ask a follow-up question, but was beaten to it by a man from an Italian newspaper who asked how many officers were involved in the search.

More questions followed and Cali called on Lombardo and the mayor to answer some of them. He also wanted to demonstrate that the various departments were working together on this.

He found the whole process gruelling and stressful. And it was made worse by the fact that a persistent voice in his head was telling him that the bomb at the basilica was just the beginning.

Chapter Thirteen

For forty-four of his sixty-two years Giuseppe Rosselli had been a gondolier. His "beat" was the lower part of the Grand Canal and his sleek black gondola was always moored next to a restaurant terrace almost directly opposite the Venetian baroque church of Santa Maria Della Salute.

Throughout the year he would labour back and forth along the many canals, resplendent in his distinctive straw hat and red-striped T-shirt.

Some days were slacker than others and before the tourist season was in full swing there were occasions when only one or two people, usually Americans and Japanese, were prepared to fork out the high price of a gondola ride.

This was going to be one of those days, he thought, as he busied himself by tidying up the deck. It was hardly likely that people would be in the mood to go on a joyride through the city, after they'd been warned of the possibility that more bombs could go off.

He sat down for a rest and a smoke and the gondola bobbed up and down on the swell created by a passing vaporetto. He watched it chug up the Grand Canal. Then he lit the cigarette and was just about to inhale when something caught his eye.

It was a small thing, and had it not been for the fact that he knew this little corner of Venice so well, it probably would have gone unnoticed. But he knew he hadn't seen it before, whatever it was.

It was disc-shaped and seemed to be about fifteen inches wide by a few inches thick. It was attached to the underside of the crowded restaurant terrace which itself was about four feet above the water.

He stared at the object for some seconds before something registered in his brain and he sat bolt upright.

Then he tried to compose his thoughts and at the same time make some conscious effort to still the wings of the butterflies in his stomach. It wasn't easy. He had a good idea now what the object was and it frightened him. What was it the Carabinieri Colonel had said over the radio? Don't approach anything that looks suspicious. Just get to a phone and inform the police.

Sound advice, he thought, as he reached in his pocket for his cell.

The police arrived within minutes. Two launches filled to overflowing with uniforms pulled up next to the gondola. Others came on foot along the quayside and they wasted no time clearing people away from the area. A couple of shops were evacuated, along with the restaurant.

A Carabinieri officer extracted the relevant facts from Giuseppe, who was more than anxious now to get his precious gondola out of harm's way. But after he had parted with the details the officer said that he would have to leave the gondola where it was for the time being.

"But the gondola is my livelihood," Giuseppe protested. "Without it I am nothing."

"And if I allow you to return to it and the bomb goes off?" the officer said.

"It is a chance I am prepared to take."

"Well, I'm not. Now, please, get back. We're only trying to help."

Another launch pulled up against the quayside and two of the men who stepped from it were wearing the distinctive blue overalls of the bomb disposal squad. They walked briskly ahead of a small group of Carabinieri to the restaurant entrance.

In a few minutes the bomb disposal men emerged on the terrace. All eyes were on them. They walked to the edge of the terrace and peered down into the water. Then one of them climbed over the balustrade and lowered himself down a short iron step ladder.

When his feet were resting on the bottom rung he stopped. He found he was able to reach the strange looking object with his outstretched hands as he clung to the ladder using his legs. Gently, very gently, he examined it with his fingertips.

Then after a few seconds he looked up at his colleague and confirmed that the object was a mine and that the timer had been activated.

Chapter Fourteen

Activity in the operation room became even more frenetic when the Italian Prime Minister announced on television that he was rushing to Venice to offer his support. Cali wasn't entirely surprised. This thing was too big to ignore, especially when an election was only a couple of months away.

The pressure was immense, and back behind his desk Cali was forced to down a couple of pain killers to combat a raging headache.

The scene he'd witnessed in St Mark's Square and the subsequent press conference had left him feeling anxious and helpless. He was trying not to show it, but it wasn't easy. He was not in control of events and he couldn't be sure how the crisis would develop. The uncertainty was making it hellishly difficult to formulate an effective response to what had happened.

For the first time Cali wished he had never been promoted to his current position with the Carabinieri. The weight of responsibility on his shoulders was almost overwhelming. He did not want to be the person making the decisions, but that was where he was at. He was the officer calling the shots, which meant that he would also be the one to carry the can if things went wrong.

He was already doubting his own judgement in revealing so much at the press conference. Telling the media that a search was under way for more bombs had sent them into a frenzy. The phones hadn't stopped ringing. The TV news presenters were sounding like prophets of doom. One even quoted a 'source' within police headquarters as saying that there was evidence that dozens of bombs had been planted in the city. But Cali had declined to confirm this.

So far there was no widespread panic, but reports were reaching him that the causeway linking Venice to the mainland was much busier than usual.

Cali was still hoping and praying that Barone had planted just the one device in the naïve belief that it would be enough to make the authorities acquiesce to his demand.

But this ray of hope faded the moment the call came in informing him that a gondolier had discovered a limpet mine.

*

"That confirms it," Cali said, his face ashen. "The bastard was telling the truth in his letter."

Cali had convened an urgent meeting with Lombardo, the mayor and various other officials. The atmosphere in his office was tense. The news that a limpet mine had been discovered had alarmed everyone.

The timing device had shown that it had been due to detonate at 3:pm – which meant it was not one of the two that, according to Barone's note, would explode at 1:pm, four hours after the first.

The device was at the lab being checked over, but initial reports suggested that it was powerful enough to have caused serious damage had it gone off as planned.

Cali thought of all the people who might have been on the restaurant terrace at the time and his blood ran cold. Another tragedy had been avoided by an amazing stroke of luck.

Lombardo looked at his watch and said, "The second and third bombs are due to go off in an hour."

Cali felt his chest tighten and for a moment he couldn't catch his breath. He needed to silence the noise in his head in order to think. But that was proving impossible. It was like the whole world was demanding answers he didn't have and the stress of it was burning up the oxygen in his lungs.

He leaned forward and buried his face in his sweaty palms. He had never been so tired nor so scared and found himself gritting his teeth so hard his gums ached.

He got up and stepped across the room to where a large plan of the city was pinned to the wall. The layout was in yellow and through it was an inverted S, blue in colour, that represented the Grand Canal.

Countless other canals were shown in blue, flowing between famous buildings and landmarks. Over to the left was the railway station and the causeway across to Mestra. The Grand Canal flowed downwards, under the Rialto bridge, past the Accademia and out into the basin.

A unique place was Venice, Cali thought. One of a kind. A masterpiece of human achievement. Only an insane mind could ever think of destroying it.

Barone's letter said that after the second and third explosions seventeen more devices would go off at irregular intervals up until midnight. And then between midnight and 3:am no less than forty bombs would explode at the same time. If that happened then Venice was doomed. The damage would be on a colossal scale. It was a horrifying thought.

The phone rang. He sat down and lifted the receiver.

"Cali here."

"I've been trying to get through to you all morning."

It was Susanna and the sound of her voice warmed him from within. It reminded him that he wasn't alone. Even though she wasn't here beside him she would be sharing his agony through every interminable second.

"How are you?" he asked.

"All the better now that I've finally got through to you."

"I'm sorry. It's been hell down here."

"I can imagine."

"Did you catch the press conference?"

"Yes. I didn't realise it was so serious. You should have told me."

"I couldn't. Where are the boys?"

"Right here with me. When they heard you were on TV they came rushing home. They're sulking now because I won't let them out again."

"Let them sulk all they want. Just keep them off the streets."

"I will." She paused. "Is it true there are more bombs?"

He couldn't very well lie to her, but at the same time he did not want to alarm her with the bitter truth.

"We think so," he said. "We'll know better in a little while."

There was a moment of silence. Then she said, "Are you really thinking seriously of moving everyone out of Venice?"

The question surprised him. "I'm afraid I might have to," he said.

"So it's true that we would all be safer on the mainland."

Cali closed his eyes and swivelled his chair so he was facing the window. He knew that if and when he gave the order to evacuate there would be pandemonium, despite the efforts that would be made to control the exodus, and he didn't want Susanna and the boys to be a part of it.

So he came to a decision.

"I want you to move to the mainland right now," he said, aware that everyone in the room was listening to him. "I'll arrange for a boat to pick you up in about thirty minutes. Pack only what you'll need."

"You can't be serious," she said. "I couldn't go without you."

"You can and you will, if not for me then for the boys. I'm going to have to make some important decisions in the next couple of hours and I don't want to have to worry about you."

"But…"

"No buts, please. Just do as I ask and be ready when the boat arrives."

She started sobbing and he wished he could go home and see her before she went.

"Everything will be all right," he said.

"Oh, Armond, I'm scared. Who is doing this to our city? What sort of madman is he?"

"There's no time to go into that now. I just want a promise from you that you'll leave on the boat I'm sending."

"I promise. But please be careful."

"I will."

"I love you."

"I love you too."

Cali hung up and as he stared out the window at the brilliant blue of the sky he felt the tears well up in his eyes. He sat like that until the moment of emotion had passed, then turned and faced the others.

"If more bombs go off at one o'clock I'll immediately announce a mandatory evacuation of the city," he said. "I leave it open to you all to make similar arrangements for your families. And bear in mind that you'll do your jobs better without having to fear for their safety."

Lombardo said, "I confess I'm guilty of having taken such precautions already. My wife is now on her way to relatives in Mestra."

"You needn't feel ashamed," Cali said. "We wouldn't be human if we didn't think of our loved ones first."

"Quite," the mayor said. "And I'll gladly follow suit. As you know I haven't a wife now, but I do have a daughter. This boat you send for your wife can stop at my daughter's home on the way. I'll call her and tell her to be ready with her children."

"That's good," Cali said. Then he gave a weary sigh and added, "Now I suppose all we can do is hope and pray that it doesn't get as bad as we fear it will."

Chapter Fifteen

The young Italian clerk had been perfect prey for Cristina Perri. It became clear after several weeks of observation by the New Red Brigades that he enjoyed the company of girls. He was a frequent visitor to Venice's late night clubs and tried hard to strike up with a different girl each time. He didn't always make out, though, and often he would return to his apartment alone and slightly the worse through drink.

"We think we've found someone who can help you get a job in the building," Marsella had told her. "His name is Roberto Russo. You'll probably like him since he must be one of the horniest bastards in the city. You shouldn't have any trouble getting him to take you home. From there on it will be up to you."

That was five weeks ago. Then a few days later she went to a club just off the Mercerie to meet him. Cristina wore a flimsy white silk dress that clung to her flesh like wet paper and Marsella told her she looked sensational. He went with her to the club and pointed the mark out to her, then left her to it.

Cristina was pleased to discover that Roberto was an extremely sexy man. He had good Latin looks and a shock of thick black hair that curled around the ears. He was wearing an open-neck white shirt and tight trousers that were designed to show exactly what was on offer underneath. He was there by himself and had yet to strike up a conversation with any of the women. So she wasted no time moving in.

She went straight up to him at the bar and said, "Like to dance?"

He stared at her, unable to conceal his surprise. She smiled, grabbed his hand, and led him onto the postage-stamp floor.

They were playing a slow number and she was able to get in close. As they danced she moved her thigh between his legs, gently caressing the growing lump in his trousers.

"You have a delicious body," Cristina whispered into his ear and she could feel the sweat break out on his cheek. "I would give anything to see you naked."

Naturally he couldn’t believe his luck. He started shaking and she could feel it. It pleased her immensely to think that she could turn on a man as easily as this. But then it had always been so, ever since she was a teenager in Naples.

An hour later they left the club and wandered through the silent streets of Venice, he with his arm around her shoulder, she with her hand clutching his backside. They went to his apartment, a tiny self-contained affair overlooking a small canal, and there they made urgent, passionate love. He was good, she thought, much better than she had expected, and she did her best to make him happy, which wasn't difficult because it took very little to please him.

Afterwards they lay on his bed in the dark and talked. He revealed to her what little there was to reveal about himself and she told him a pack of lies. How she had moved to Venice from Rome and was now looking for a job. How her parents had both been killed in the same auto accident when she was seventeen. He took it all in, poor gullible bastard.

"Now all I have to do is find a job," she was saying. "If I don't I may soon have to return home."

"What kind of job are you looking for?"

"I'm an all-round office assistant," she lied. "I have secretarial skills and I'm computer literate. I'm also very good at what I do. I don't suppose there are any jobs at your police station."

"I'm not sure. I could check."

She beamed a smile at him "You would do that for me?"

"Sure I would."

She leaned over and kissed him, long and hard. "Can you imagine what fun we'd have if we worked in the same building?"

He laughed. "I'll speak to someone first thing in the morning."

The next afternoon he called to tell her they needed to fill three admin positions on a temporary basis and he would be happy to arrange an interview.

"You're such a sweetheart," she told him. "And you can be sure that if I'm taken on your life is going to change for the better."

*

Now Cristina was about to spend yet another lunch hour in Roberto's office on the first floor of the municipal police building. This would probably be the last time though, which was a pity because it was an event she had come to look forward to each day.

Their relationship was purely a physical one. They enjoyed each other's flesh and that was as far as it went. Aside from the obligatory small talk they rarely spoke, but it was an arrangement that suited them both.

When she entered Roberto's office he was sitting behind his desk. It amused her to think that he was completely oblivious to the fact that in a storage room along the corridor she had hidden a small homemade bomb. Soon the timer would be activated and an explosion would rip a hole in the side of the building leading to its evacuation.

She could hardly wait.

Without being asked she closed the door behind her and locked it with the key. As she walked towards him she glanced at her watch. Five minutes to one. Zero hour. She felt a tingling of excitement.

"You're early," he said, rising to his feet. "Which is just as well. I've got to cut it short today. There's a lot on."

She was already unbuttoning her blouse.

"It's this business over the bombs," he said. "Everybody's going crazy. With so many people out looking for the damn things its left us short here."

Her blouse dropped to the floor. She reached her hand behind her and unclipped her bra.

"Here, let me," he said and took it from her.

Very gently he ran his fingers over her breasts, then her shoulders, then the flatness of her stomach. He took her left nipple in his mouth, savouring its tautness with his tongue. At the same time he lowered his hands and unbuckled her trousers.

When he was free of his shirt he threw it haphazardly to one side. Then he ripped off his own trousers and underpants with such haste he almost tripped over the tangle of clothes.

He pulled her to him and kissed her, pressing his tongue deep into her mouth. She responded with an urgency that she hadn't experienced before. It wasn't solely because he was a good lover. Her senses were heightened by the fact that a couple more devices were about to blow hell out of Venice. That was a thrill in itself. Indeed, in the past she had attained a peculiar kind of sexual satisfaction from knowing that she was partly responsible for the various acts of terrorism the New Red Brigades had committed.

"Over at the window," she was saying. "I want you to come at me from behind."

He followed her over to the open window and she leaned on the ledge so her breasts were hidden from outside by the sill. Below her the little square was packed with people.

Roberto freed her of her panties and began to run his fingers gently along the length of her spine and between her buttocks.

"Now, Roberto," she urged, knowing it was almost one. "Now, now."

In a moment he was inside her and thrusting feverishly, a gasp of pleasure emerging from his parted lips. Almost there, she was thinking. Any second now.

"I'm going to come," Roberto yelled and at the same time there was an explosion in the city and a huge mushroom of black billowing smoke rose above the rooftops.

"Don't stop," she cried. "Go on. Go on."

He did but with less enthusiasm than before and when the second blast happened in another part of the city he just froze, unable to continue even though he was so near to a climax.

Cristina kept going, though, and when finally she was there she let out a gasp of pleasure that would have been heard in the square below if it hadn't been for all the commotion.

Chapter Sixteen

The first of the two explosions shook all the furniture in Cali's office. Even the chair he was sitting on moved a couple of inches across the floor.

He hurried over to the window. At first he could see nothing, then, rising into the sky beyond the church of San Zaccaria, he saw the smoke.

He was still looking when the second explosion rocked the city. It wasn't so close, but it was just as loud and as he stood at the window a cold hand began clawing at his heart.

A minute passed and the phone rang. Lombardo, who had been pacing the room, snatched it up and listened. When he replaced the receiver, he said, “The first explosion was at the Church of San Giorgio dei Greci. Apparently the tower has collapsed across the canal on top of a passing vaporetto."

Cali closed his eyes. He couldn't believe this was really happening.

"That was my own office," Lombardo added. "They actually saw it happen."

Cali recalled that the Questura was close to the church, on the opposite side of a canal. The church tower was a distinctive feature of the Venice skyline because of the way it had always leaned to one side. It was the perfect target for terrorists as even a small bomb could conceivably have brought it crashing down.

The phone rang a second time. Lombardo lifted the receiver and listened, his face clouding.

"Now get over there and find out the full extent of the damage," he ordered, before slamming the phone down. "The Hotel Luna. First reports say a huge chunk has been blown out of it and there are casualties."

Cali felt a sour taste of bile in his stomach. Jesus, he thought, this is so bad.

He turned to the mayor who was sitting in a chair with tears in his eyes.

"It's time to evacuate," Cali said. "We can't hold off any longer."

The mayor nodded without speaking, pulled himself to his feet and walked out of the room like a man in a trance.

"I can't spare the time to go and see for myself what's happened," Cali said to Lombardo. "Will you keep me informed? I'll leave it up to you to co-ordinate the emergency services."

"Will do," Lombardo answered crisply.

Cali went to the door, threw it open and yelled for Mario, who appeared in a flash.

"Get the media over here now," Cali said. "Tell them I'm going to order an evacuation. That should hurry them up."

When Cali turned back into the room Lombardo was holding the phone. "My people say the vaporetto was smashed in two by the church tower. At least four bodies can be seen floating in the canal. It's also believed there were several people on the quayside directly below the church when the tower crumbled."

"My God."

"Yes, yes," Lombardo said into the phone." I see. Well keep me informed." He turned back to Cali. "Someone who saw the vaporetto pass below the Questura just before the explosion says there were about fifteen people on board. Quite a few have apparently come out of it alive. They're being pulled out of the water now."

"Do we know what it's like at the Luna?"

"Not yet. I expect a call any second."

Cali sank into his chair, shoulders slumped forward. Air gushed out of him like a punctured balloon. His skull was suddenly on fire.

The phone rang again. Lombardo listened for a moment, then turned to Cali. "The situation at the Luna looks bad. Several people are believed to be buried under the rubble. The bomb was hidden somewhere inside. It blasted the reception area."

Cali raised his arm and brought his hand crashing down on the desk top. "We could have avoided this," he yelled. "If only we'd cleared everybody out after that first explosion at the basilica."

"That's ridiculous," Lombardo said. "We've done all that could have been expected of us. There was no way we could have foreseen this. For all we knew the letter might have been a hoax. We had to wait."

"But because we held off more people have died."

“It’s not your fault, Armond.”

“I wish I could believe that,” Cali said.

The door swung open and Mario came in. "It's all arranged, sir. The media will be here in thirty minutes. Will you be ready?"

"I'm ready now. When they arrive just wheel them straight into the conference room."

Fifteen minutes later the mayor returned with news about the evacuation plan.

"To begin with we're setting up emergency reception centres in Mestra, Caposile, Portegrancli and Marghera," he said. "Food and bedding is on its way along with military detachments. We're getting help from the army and the navy."

"Sounds good," Cali said.

"We'll tour the city with magaphones for the benefit of those who aren't aware what's happening," the mayor said. "We're now in the process of commandeering everything that floats and there will be a number of departure points to which people will be directed depending where they live."

"What about those people in the hospitals and elderly folk who can't make it alone?"

"They'll get priority," the mayor said. "The hospitals will be the first public buildings to be evacuated and my office is drawing up a list of elderly people who will need help. Officers can call on them individually."

Cali nodded, satisfied. "You've done well, Mr Mayor."

"Let's just hope it's enough," the mayor said. "What about the bombs? Are we still able to continue the search for them?"

"Not now," Cali said. "Every available officer will be needed to control the crowds. Once we've cleared most of the people we'll have another go, but if we're approaching midnight I don't intend to risk their lives by making them stay."

"Do we know if there's any threat to those people on the islands and on the Lido?" the mayor asked.

It was a point Cali hadn't considered. The Venetian lagoon is littered with tiny inhabited islands and the Lido, that long strip of land that keeps the sea at bay. He took out Barone's note and read it through yet again.

"There's no mention of the islands in the letter," he said. "He refers only to Venice and the city. I think it's safe to assume that those people can stay where they are, at least for the time being."

The door opened and Mario poked his head into the room. "The press and TV people are here, sir."

Chapter Seventeen

Ten minutes later Cali was back at the lectern in front of the assembled media. Beads of sweat had gathered in the creases of his brow and he could feel the muscles in his chest getting tight.

After a long pause, he said, “This is a very sad day for our beloved city. Following the latest explosions I can confirm that at least sixteen people have been killed. We now fear that the terrorist who planted those devices may well have planted many more. I can't go into the details now about the methods and aims of this lunatic, but I will tell you that he is dead and therefore not able to reveal to us where other devices are concealed.”

There came an audible gasp from his audience. Several people started asking questions but he waved them down and carried on.

"We’ve had little luck so far in our search for the bombs,” he said. “In fact we’ve found only one. For this reason I’ve decided that the city must be evacuated."

He paused again to let his words sink in, then swallowed a huge lump before continuing.

"The decision has not been taken lightly,” he said. “We had hoped that it wouldn't come to this, but we really have no choice if we’re to safeguard the public. I'm told everything is now ready and in a moment the mayor himself will explain what should be done. We want to avoid panic situations. Arrangements have been made to clear the city as quickly and efficiently as possible.

"Everyone should stay calm and conduct themselves in an orderly way. Police officers and military personnel will be on hand to help out. People should only take with them small personal belongings as we can't afford to use up valuable space on boats.

"This of course raises the question of property in museums and art galleries. Since boats are to be commandeered to be used to transport people to the mainland it grieves me to say that space cannot be made available for even our most valued treasures. But as soon as is practicable efforts will be made to move all antiquities."

Cali knew that this last statement wouldn't go down very well in many quarters. But his primary concern was for people and not property. One life was worth a thousand works of art and he felt that he would be failing in his duty if we allowed the removal of antiquities to disrupt the outflow of people.

"Please believe me when I say that you will all be safer outside the city," he said. "Reception centres are being set up on the mainland and everything will be done to make you comfortable. I'll now let the mayor speak to you in detail about the evacuation plan."

When attention switched to the mayor, Cali got up and hurried out of the room to where Lombardo and Mario were waiting in the outer office.

Mario had a phone to his ear and as soon as he saw Cali he thrust out the handset.

“It’s the Prime Minister on the line, sir,” he said.

Cali had met the PM on two occasions in the past, both official functions in the city. He had little time for the man and considered him to be a lightweight politician who would struggle to pull the country out to the doldrums. But he appreciated the call nonetheless.

"Hello, Colonel,” the PM said. “I want you to know that I’m on my way to Venice to offer support. I’ve already ordered a hundred more troops into Mestra to help out. If you need anything else just ask."

"Thank you, sir,” Cali said.

The PM paused, then said, "I suppose you are sure, beyond all reasonable doubt, that this man Barone was acting independently of an organisation. I mean, there's no chance that someone helped him to plant the bombs is there? Someone with whom we could negotiate."

Cali wiped a hand across his sweaty brow and said, "There’s no evidence to suggest that anyone else was involved with him in the planting of the bombs, sir."

"So the situation we face is this. Over fifty more bombs are believed to be hidden in the city and seventeen will go off between now and midnight. Then between midnight and three am another forty will explode simultaneously."

"That's what the letter said."

The PM cleared his throat. “I expect I'll soon start to feel pressure from the big insurance companies and state museums. Naturally they'll be concerned about your remarks concerning the city's treasures."

Cali could feel the anger rising in him. "Are you asking me if there's anything I can do about it, sir?"

"Is there?"

"The answer is no. Everything that floats is being used to carry people. We don't have the vessels or the manpower to move tons of antiquities. Not only would it slow down the evacuation, but it would call for a massive security operation which would be impossible to mount in the circumstances."

"What about after all the people have been evacuated? Could they move the treasures out then?"

“I’m not sure there’ll be time, sir. Our deadline is midnight. By then we need to have the city clear of people.”

“Very well,” the PM said. “Just carry on what you’re doing. You have my full support. I look forward to seeing you when I arrive."

Chapter Eighteen

As was only to be expected there were those who were not prepared to heed the advice about staying calm and doing as they'd been asked. One group of about thirty people from an office block near the Rialto Bridge stormed past a queue and onto a vaporetto landing stage.

Order was restored by a Carabinieri officer who fired a burst into the air from his handgun and shouted a warning that he was prepared to use it on people if he was forced to.

Another fight broke out along the Fondamenta della Zattere when a crowd of people attempted to board a visiting ship carrying a Panamanian flag. They were beaten back by the crew using sticks.

There was chaos at the station and the huge car park in the Piazzale Roma. Too many people were trying to squeeze onto the trains, causing delays in departure. In the car park there was pandemonium because everyone tried to leave at once to cross the causeway and this resulted in the police having to come and sort out the mess.

By 1:55pm, one hour after the mayor had finished his talk on the air, some eight thousand people had left Venice for the mainland. At each of the twenty-three official departure points huge crowds quickly formed and the police and army had their hands full keeping the people in line.

Boats of all shapes and sizes moved in a continuous line along the Grand Canal. People were crammed into vaporetti, motor boats and gondolas. There was a loud and constant chorus of sirens across the city.

In the ninety miles of narrow alleys that wind through Venice people dashed in all directions, without thought for each other. There were instances of children being pushed to the ground and trampled on.

At 2:00pm the fourth bomb exploded. It had been left lying under a bush against the wall of an apartment block just off the Via Garibaldi. The blast ripped a hole in the side of the building and reduced three homes to rubble. Luckily most of the occupants of the block had already left and the only person to die was an old man who had refused to leave.

The affect the blast had on the departing population was significant as the sound of the explosion was heard throughout the city. At some of the departure points police suddenly found themselves confronted by panic-stricken mobs.

At the landing stage on the Fondamenta Nouve so many people scrambled onto a water bus on hearing the blast that it keeled dangerously to one side, throwing dozens into the water.

At 3:45pm Cali got his first report from official observers who were monitoring the progress of the evacuation. It said that about 30,000 people had so far left the city.

Three people were known to have died in the chaos, one a girl who was trampled underfoot by a mob, another a boy of twelve who fell into a canal and drowned before rescuers could reach him. The third was a middle-aged man who stumbled in the Piazza and hit his head on a step.

On the mainland a major operation was under way. Army barracks, hotels and business premises were being used as reception centres where people could get food and a bed. It was all being carried out with surprising efficiency.

Each person was asked to give his or her name so that their families would be able to trace them. Some had relatives or friends to put them up and this helped to ease the burden on the authorities. Fleets of coaches began transporting thousands of people out of Mestra to outlying towns.

There was looting very early on in Venice, although on a minor scale. A gang of youths smashed the windows of a jewellers shop and grabbed handfuls of rings and bracelets.

Another looter wasn't so lucky. He attempted to steal a priceless painting from the Accadamia before it was shut to the public. He pulled it down from its mounting and ran for the entrance with alarm bells blaring about him. He was stopped by two burly security guards who brought him down without causing any damage to the picture.

The Carabinieri station became the operations centre. Cali stayed in his office throughout, helping Lombardo to coordinate the emergency services and generally being on hand to make the decisions.

The mayor worked from the same office so as to aid communication and from there he kept in touch by telephone with the officers who were organising things outside on a district by district basis.

Maps of Venice, Mestra, Portegrandi and Caposile were pinned to the walls and red flags indicated the departure points and reception centres and blue flags the bombs and mines that had already gone off.

The phone rang just before 6:pm and Lombardo answered it. When the call ended, he said, "That makes six gone and fifty-four to go."

"What do you mean?"

"Your men just found a limpet mine attached to a pole beneath the Palazzo Goner Contarini on the Grand Canal. They've managed to diffuse it."

Chapter Nineteen

Marsella, Scalise and Greco had watched Cali's press conference on the TV in a bar on Calle Fuseri. The place had been crowded with locals, but while Cali spoke they were all silent. After he'd finished, most of them left the bar and their unfinished drinks and hurried home.

The three terrorists walked out after the broadcast and strolled casually westwards. The streets were full of worried people rushing towards the water bus stops or heading north to the causeway and station.

The three men arrived at Campo Santo and here the police were very much in evidence. The large building housing the municipal police headquarters was at one end of the square. Because it was a modern concrete structure it stood out from the rest.

"Here she comes," Marsella said and the others turned towards the entrance to the building from where Cristina Rebaldo had just emerged.

"Right on time as usual," Scalise observed with a smile.

Cristina walked towards them with all the grace of a professional model. She wore tight-fitting beige trousers and a brown sweater.

"Hello, Cristina," Marsella said when she reached them.

“I have only a few minutes” she said. “The situation is chaotic inside the building."

They strolled towards a nearby canal. When they came to the water's edge they stopped and Cristina looked back over her shoulder at the police headquarters.

Marsella said, "So update me, Cristina. Is everything in place?"

Cristina nodded. “They plan for the station to remain fully functional as long as possible. They’re talking about leaving a skeleton staff on duty even after the evacuation.”

“Just as we thought they might,” Marsella said. “Have you set the timer on the bomb?”

“Of course. It’s in a storage room on the first floor and will take out the south facing wall and bring the floor down on some ground-level offices. “

“Perfect,” Marsella said. “After that there’s no way they’ll leave anyone inside.”

Cristina smiled. “Which will leave the way open for us to move in.”

Chapter Twenty

For Paul and Jennifer Hayward it was an upsetting end to an otherwise perfect honeymoon. For nearly two weeks they had wallowed in their love for one another, a love that seemed to be enriched by the fact that they were in Venice.

It seemed inconceivable that they should now be standing outside the Hotel Danieli, without their belongings, waiting to be transported to the mainland along with thousands of other people.

Paul was still trying to comfort his young wife who, on hearing the fourth explosion, had broken down in a paroxysm of tears. Like everyone else she was scared, and she was a woman who found it difficult to control her emotions.

"Come on love," Paul was saying. "Pull yourself together. We'll be all right. At least we'll soon be clear of here."

"I'm frightened, Paul."

"I know, but there's no need to be. Nothing's going to happen to us."

She found comfort in his words and realised for the first time just how dependent on him she had become. Before this moment she hadn't thought about it. In the past she had been so independent. A girl who spoke her own mind and did her own thing.

The realisation that she now had a husband without whom she wouldn't want to go on living came as quite a shock.

"Not long now," Paul said.

For twenty minutes they had been queuing to get on one of the departing boats. They were now on the landing stage and there were hundreds of people behind them being kept in line by policemen. The only luggage they'd been allowed to bring was Jennifer's small overnight bag and into this they'd stuffed everything of value.

Jennifer wiped her eyes with a handkerchief and said, "I've got to go to the loo, Paul."

"You can't go now," Paul said. "We'll be on the next boat."

"It isn't here yet. I shan't be long."

"OK, but hurry. We don't want to stay here any longer than we have to. I'll hold our place."

Jennifer went quickly into the Hotel Danieli where they had been staying at enormous expense. She hurried through the plush reception area to the toilets. After relieving herself, she left the toilet at a run and was back out front in no time at all. She saw immediately that the boat was pulling alongside the landing stage and Paul was in the group that would be boarding it. She ran towards him and he began to wave at her from the far end of the stage.

She raised her arm to wave back, but in that instant there was a loud explosion and the end part of the landing stage went up in a huge cloud of swirling black smoke at the centre of which was a flash of orange. Jennifer watched, horrified, as her husband and several other people got swallowed up by it.

A large body of people swarmed past her towards the relative safety of the buildings set back from the water. Women were screaming, children crying and policemen were shouting orders to each other and not being heard above the cacophony of noise.

When the smoke cleared Jennifer stared in disbelief at the landing stage. There was a big hole in the wooden boards where previously people had been standing. Most of them had been blown into the water or onto the empty boat which had also suffered considerable damage.

But she could see her husband quite clearly. He had been thrown back along the landing stage and he was sprawled out on his back with one leg up against the wall of the ferry office. Even from where she stood she could see the dreadful extent of his injuries.

His right arm was hanging on by a shred and the other was a mass of blood. But what most appalled her, and indeed caused her to faint, was the fact that he no longer had a face.

Chapter Twenty One

By 7:pm the death toll had risen to twenty-eight. Two more bombs had exploded in the two hours since the one that killed four people on the landing stage. The first had damaged an office building in Santo Stefano and the second had gone off in an empty shop in the Rialto market, killing a passer-by.

As the blitz continued so did the evacuation. Thousands of people were ferried to the mainland and the canals were crammed with boats.

Cali monitored the progress from his office, his senses in disarray, his mind overwhelmed by the sheer scale of the operation they had undertaken. He was still struggling to come to terms with what was happening. The view from his window filled his heart with despair. It was like a war zone out there. His city was under siege and the people were fleeing for their lives.

For years the authorities had discussed various doomsday scenarios, including what would happen if the entire city faced being submerged under water. But never had they considered the possibility of having to organise a mass exodus because of a series of bombs planted by an insane terrorist.

It was the stuff of nightmares.

And soon he would have to decide what was to be done when the evacuation was completed. So far eight bombs had exploded and two had been diffused, which left fifty still to go off.

Already irreparable damage had been done to the city. He would soon have to give the order for patrols to start searching again in the hope that at least some of the devices could be found.

But it was unlikely that they would achieve much in the little time they had. Well before midnight he would be forced to withdraw all the police and military personnel. He had thought of leaving small teams in the city, but had come to the conclusion that it wouldn't be fair to expect anyone to remain.

"Colonel. Are you all right?"

Cali had been totally absorbed in his thoughts. He hadn't noticed Salvatore enter the room and approach his desk.

“What is it?" he said.

"Message from the lab, sir. No fingerprints, other than those of our men, were found on the unexploded mines."

"It was only to be expected," Cali said, disappointed but not surprised.

"There's something else, sir."

“Oh?”

"I've just had a message from the mainland about a Carabinieri officer named Rienzo. Two nights ago he was badly beaten and left for dead."

"Yes, I remember. Go on."

"Well he was unconscious up until the early hours of this morning. Gradually during the day his senses have returned and in the last hour we’ve managed to interview him."

"So?"

"Well he's just told officers that he was attacked by two men who were acting suspiciously on the landing stage next to the Ponte del Vin."

"I'm sorry Salvatore. I fail to see the significance."

"It's this, sir. The landing stage in question is the one which was blasted into oblivion less than an hour ago."

Cali suddenly sat bolt upright, his mouth gaping.

"Did you say two men?"

"That's right, sir."

"Did Rienzi get a good look at them?"

"Only one of them. According to the officer who interviewed him the description does not fit Barone. He said the man was taller and younger looking. He had beside him on the landing stage a small black bag."

Cali was shaking from head to foot with excitement.

"Of course it could be a coincidence," Salvatore said.

Cali shook his head. "Somehow I don't think so. Look, get back onto the mainland, or better still go across yourself and get a fuller description and any other details from Rienzi. And step on it, Salvatore. We haven't much time."

Cali summoned Lombardo and the mayor from the operations centre and gave them the news.

"It must have been Barone with another man," he said. "Which means he wasn't working alone."

"But how can we prove it?" Lombardo asked.

"We don't have to prove it. We act on the assumption that there is after all at least one other person who knows where the devices are. Our task now is to find him"

"That won't be easy," the mayor said.

Cali turned to Lombardo. "Get onto the PM's office and inform him of this development."

As Lombardo stood up to reach for the phone a lot of things happened at once. Outside there was a deafeningly loud explosion. The office window exploded and glass flew like shrapnel. Shards blew across the room, embedding themselves in flesh and furniture. In the same moment the lower part of the wall to Lombardo's right caved in, bringing down the rest of the wall on top of it.

The force of the blast knocked all three men to the floor. Cali was blown out of his seat and across the carpet to the far wall where a small cabinet fell on top of him, rendering him unconscious.

The mayor was thrown on his face with a heavy thud and a piece of glass gouged a chunk out of his right arm.

Lombardo took the brunt of it, though. He'd been standing with his back to the window and was hit by the full thrust of the blast. The entire length of his body was badly scorched and small shards of glass clung to his clothes like struggling insects.

The fragment that killed him was six inches long with a point as sharp as a needle. It struck to the back of his head, went straight through the skull, and became wedged inside his brain.

Chapter Twenty Two

The terrorists were back at the flat drinking wine and discussing how well things were going.

The excitement was such that Greco proposed a toast to his grandfather.

"If not for him this would not be happening," he announced.

The old man had died in that faraway hospital bed almost a year ago. In his mind's eye Greco saw again the white hair and sunken eyes; the wrinkled flesh and withered body.

His grandfather had at one time been one of Venice's most respected traders. But on that day he was a sad, broken man, a shadow of the person he once was.

Greco had been shocked at the sight of the old man's face as it stared up at him from between the crisp, white sheets of the hospital bed. In the seven years since he had last seen his grandfather he seemed to have aged an eternity. No longer were the eyes clear and wide and alert. No longer did his flesh have that healthy outdoor look which had so impressed the ladies. Now his face was pale, the leathery skin shrivelled over protruding bones, and his eyes were devoid of any kind of expression. He looked like a hideous figure made out of wax which had begun to melt. His heart was giving out on him and the doctors gave him only a few days at the most.

Greco had sat on the chair next to the bed and it seemed to require a tremendous effort on the part of the old man to turn his head gradually towards him.

For several long seconds the old man did not move. And then a flicker of recognition showed on his face. He spoke in a voice that was surprisingly clear. "Vittore, how did you find me?" he said.

Greco leaned forward. "The hospital managed to trace me. They say I'm your only living relative."

"I did not ask them to look for you. I would have been content to die alone."

Ungrateful bastard, Greco thought, immediately regretting having come.

The old man's lips parted in what could only be construed as a smile. He said, "There is no money, if that is why you have come. Surely you can tell from the look of me that I will die a pauper."

Greco couldn't help but laugh. He had come purely out of a sense of duty to a man he had known and loved as a boy.

"I thought that after all these years people would have forgotten about the story of the gold," the old man said. "Obviously I was wrong."

Greco had indeed forgotten about it until now. He was just a boy when the old man was sent to prison and the rumour spread all over Venice. They said he had killed his best friend and business partner Albert Pelli because the two couldn't agree what should be done with a hoard of Nazi gold they had found which was reckoned to be worth millions of American dollars. Greco's father had told him years later that the rumour had been put about by Pelli's wife who had been forced to admit that she did not know where the gold was or where it had come from. Only that it existed and was the reason why her husband had been brutally murdered.

But throughout the trial and the subsequent ten-year prison sentence the old man had emphatically denied all knowledge of so-called Nazi gold. He had maintained that he had stabbed his partner to death during a fight over the running of the business. As far as Greco could discover there was no evidence to suggest otherwise. After all, would a man who had a hidden treasure live out his life in relative poverty?

"What makes you think I've come because of that ridiculous story?" Greco asked him.

"Why else would you come?" the old man said. "I'm surprised you didn't ask me about it sooner. Like all those other vultures who believed the rumours and pestered me for years."

Greco shook his head. "You talk as if you actually believe in the gold yourself."

"And that surprises you?"

"After you've denied it for so long. What do you think? I'm sure that if you had managed to lay your hands on a Nazi treasure trove you wouldn't be finishing your days in this God forsaken place."

The old man stared thoughtfully at the ceiling, his bared chest rising and falling with every breath. A tear escaped from his left eye and crept through the stubble towards his ear.

Greco said, "What's wrong?"

"I suppose I'm feeling sorry for myself," the old man said. "Not because I'm dying. In many ways that will be a relief. No, it's because fate has been so unfair to me over the years and this feeling of resentment I will take to my grave. Perhaps I'd feel better if I told you the truth. Then someone would know the agony I've suffered over the years."

"What are you talking about?"

"The gold, Vittore. I'm talking about the gold. After all, that is why you are here isn't it?"

"But there is no gold."

The old man managed a weak smile. "Oh, but there is, Vittore. It was always there. From the very beginning."

Greco stared at him. "If that's true then why did you lie about it and why the hell have you been poor all these years?"

"I lied because I did not want people to know the gold existed," the old man said. "I was hoping that one day, when I was released from prison, I would retrieve it and use it to make up for those ten lost years. But something happened which prevented me from being able to retrieve the gold. The final irony if you like."

"What the hell are you talking about?" Greco said.

"It's a long story, Vittore, but since I'm about to die I may as well tell it to you."

Chapter Twenty Three

June 25 1944.

Carlo Greco and his business partner Albert Pelli had spent the day in Trieste buying up stock for their little clothes shop in Venice's Campo Santos. They were driving back along the road to Mestra through the heavy wind-driven rain. It was after midnight and they were wary of running into a German patrol that would likely as not insist on searching the vehicle just for the hell of it.

For these were bad times to be out on the road so late at night. The Allies were pushing into Northern Italy and there were lots of trigger-happy Nazis about.

The two businessmen did not make the trip very often these days, once every two months usually, and only when it became necessary to restock the shop.

They were just outside Mestra when they spotted the truck in a field off to the right. They saw the broken fence and realised that there had been an accident. They pulled over and decided to investigate.

With one flashlight between them, they made their way unsteadily down the wet, slippery embankment.

The vehicle was a German army truck and part of its load, some heavy looking wooden crates, had fallen to the ground.

Albert poked the flashlight through the cab window. The sight of the two blood-splattered figures turned his stomach over. They were both in German uniform and they were much older than he was.

"What have you found?" Carlo said.

"Two men. Germans"

"Alive?"

"I can't tell from here. But I don't think so. There's no movement."

"We'd better find out. Do you think we can get them out of there?"

"We can try."

It was more difficult than it looked. Both doors had been buckled in the crash and it took a great deal of effort to wrench one of them open. When Albert climbed into the cab he saw immediately that the two occupants were dead. As quickly as he could he clambered back down, ashen faced.

"They're dead," he said. "They're pretty cold so it's my guess they've been here some time."

"What should we do?"

"We'll have to report it when we get to Mestra. They'll send someone out to clear the wreckage."

They walked around to the back of the truck and Albert pulled back the tarpaulin and shone the flashlight inside. The beam of light revealed more crates. They were the same as those lying on the grass. He turned and walked over to the nearest crate. A cursory examination with the flashlight showed that it was not labelled.

"Over here," Carlo said suddenly. "Look, this one has broken open."

"My God," Albert yelled when a moment later he saw what was inside the crate. He bent down and lifted up a heavy gold ingot in trembling hands. There was an inscription on it that told him all he needed to know.

Deutche Reichbank 1 kilo Feingold 999.9

This was part of a hoard of treasure looted by the Nazis from bank reserves and wealthy Italian Jews. For years the bastards had been melting down gold and casting it into bars with the mark of the German central bank imprinted on them.

"It's probably going south with most of the other booty our beloved Nazis have plundered whilst they've been in residence here," Carlo said bitterly. "A boat is probably waiting somewhere along the coast to take it to where the Allies won't get their hands on it."

Albert felt sicker than when he had looked upon the two dead Germans for the first time. He said, "We'll probably be shot for having seen this."

The crate contained six ingots and they counted twenty crates.

The two looked at each other and Carlo said, "If all these crates are full then there is a fortune in gold here."

"So why isn't it under guard? Surely such a valuable load should have an armed escort."

"Not necessarily," Carlo said. "That would attract the attention of the resistance who have been known to set up ambushes. This way nobody suspects anything."

For several long seconds the two men stood staring at the shining piece of metal.

Then Carlo said, "Are you thinking what I'm thinking?"

"Possibly."

"But would we get away with it?"

Both were aware that taking the gold would place them in very great danger. The Nazis, were they to find out, would show no mercy. The pair of them would probably be shot, perhaps even tortured by the Gestapo. But the thought of all that gold, all that wealth, was a temptation that was difficult to resist.

Carlo's insides were knotted. The decision had been thrust upon them too suddenly. He really needed more time to consider the consequences, to question whether he was capable of living for God knew how many years with the knowledge that people would be looking for the gold and one mistake, one uttered reference to it in the wrong place, could bring his own life to an abrupt and painful end.

He guessed that Albert was thinking along the same lines and his eyes narrowed questioningly. He said, "Well?"

Albert swallowed. His eyes darted from Carlo to the gold on the ground to the lamps of the van up on the road.

"I don't know," he said. "I mean, where would we hide all these crates for one thing?"

"What about the shop's basement?" Carlo said. "It's big enough and it's empty because of the damp."

"I don't think so. If it's ever searched by the Nazis it's the first place they'll look."

Albert smiled knowingly. "Not if we seal the entrance with a new floor."

*

It took them half an hour to load the crates onto their rented truck during which time no other vehicles came along the road. Luckily there was plenty of room on the truck even with their newly acquired stock.

They drove to Mestra and across the causeway where they parked up next to their small boat. From there they made four trips to the shop, lifting the gold in through the canal entrance.

Access to the basement was through a floor hatch in the fitting room at the back of the shop. By the time they had lowered the crates down the steps and stacked them up it was five in the morning.

They were too excited to sleep so they drank strong coffee and talked about the new floor they intended to lay across the fitting room.

As soon as the working day began they went to the hardware store and picked up enough concrete mix to do the job. By evening they'd spread it across the fitting room and next day they laid a new carpet on top.

Then they agreed not to talk about the gold and not to retrieve it until several years after the war ended.

*

"What happened?" Vittore Greco asked his grandfather.

"Three years after the war was over Albert wanted to dig up the gold," the old man said. "But I was against it because the authorities were scouring the country looking for treasure looted by the Nazis. Plus the gold was still fresh in the minds of many people who believed it was hidden in the area. I thought it was too risky.

"We argued about it for weeks until Albert decided he was going to dig up the floor regardless of what I said. We were in the shop at the time and I got in such a temper I struck him. He retaliated and we suddenly found ourselves fighting on the floor of the shop.

"Then I saw the scissors on the counter. I don't know what came over me. I picked them up in a blind rage and stabbed him again and again in the chest. He was lying dead on the floor when the door opened and a customer walked in."

"So he was killed because of the gold?" Greco said.

The old man nodded.

"That's incredible."

"But true."

"I don't disbelieve you. Now tell me what happened to the gold."

The old man coughed. Greco noticed that he looked much worse than when he had arrived. He seemed to be having to force his eyelids to stay open and his voice was losing some of its strength.

Eventually he said, "It's still there, right where we left it, only each of those gold bars is now worth fifty thousand American dollars. It means the total value is over five million dollars."

Greco was silent for a spell and his heart froze in his chest. It sounded too fantastic to be true.

"But why did you never retrieve it?" he asked.

The old man shook his head. His wrinkled face expressed a deep sadness and his rheumy eyes were dull and lifeless.

"I couldn't," he said. "Whilst I was in prison I was declared bankrupt and the shop was repossessed by the bank. It was bought up with two neighbouring properties and they were converted into a single building."

"But surely there must have been some way to get to it when you got out."

"Impossible," the old man said through pinched lips. "You see, the new building was turned into the municipal police headquarters."

"You mean the gold is buried under a fucking police station?" Greco said, aghast.

The old man nodded and gave a wry smile.

Later that evening he died.

*

Greco had thought long and hard about what his grandfather had told him. And the more he thought about it the more excited he became.

He trawled the Internet for information and spent hours researching archive material in the library. He came across documents confirming that on June 25 1944 a hoard of gold bullion was stolen from a truck on the mainland close to Venice. Crates containing over a hundred gold bars had never been recovered but there were rumours at the time that they had been hidden somewhere in the city.

During the weeks following his grandfather's death a thought settled in his mind and refused to move.

Eventually he told the story of the gold to Marsella and together they tried to come up with a plan to get at it. At first it seemed impossible.

"It's not as though it's under a house or a church in the middle of nowhere," Marsella said. "But a police station! No way. I mean, how do you blast the floor out of a police station in the middle of a city without anyone thinking it's odd?"

"The building would have to be empty," Greco said.

"Exactly. But that is never going to happen all the time the police are occupying it."

"Then we need to come up with a way to clear the building so that we can gain access and get to the gold."

“That’s about the size of it my friend,” Marsella said. “Have you got any bright ideas?”

“Actually I have,” Greco said. “But it’s pretty fucking outrageous.”

Chapter Twenty Four

Back in the present Marsella reflected on how their audacious plan had come to fruition. Months of careful planning in secret meetings. Only a select group of the most trustworthy individuals were allowed to get involved. Then the real work began.

Cristina secured a position inside the police station where she would act as their eyes and ears and plant the bomb that would help clear the building when the time was right.

The explosives were shipped to a warehouse in Mestra from various locations in northern Italy. Finally, over the past week, a number of bombs and mines were concealed in positions that had been carefully identified. Now the operation was in full flow and Marsella was delighted with the way things were going.

"At this rate the city will be deserted long before midnight," he said to Greco, who had just entered the room along with Scalise and two other men.

Marsella was standing at the window of the apartment in the Jewish quarter, watching with glee as a steady procession of people paraded along both sides of the canal below.

No one would ever suspect what was going on. How could they? The police station would simply look as though it had been one of many targets. After taking the gold they planned to detonate a second bomb there to cover their tracks.

And how easy it had been so far. Both sets of plans of the site had been simple to obtain. Those of the old clothes shop had been buried in the archives at the council offices. They were yellow and frayed, but the lines, figures and markings were clearly discernible. The plans that were prepared before the building was converted into a police station were also at the council offices. Marsella had obtained the originals of both sets from a greedy young clerk for large sums of money. The clerk was later found floating in a canal and the official death notice said he had died from drowning.

They had carefully studied the floor plans. By tracing one on top of the other they were able to tell where the old fitting room was in relation to the new building. The plans showed that the old floor, although strengthened in places with injected concrete, had been left virtually intact — a common enough procedure in Venice because of the high risk of unsettling the long established foundations. Now thick tiles had been laid on top of the concrete. Walls had been pulled down in both the shop and the apartment above it, but it was clear to see that the old fitting room had been replaced by the reception area of the police station.

"It's going better than I dared imagine it would," Greco said. "If we can pull this off people will be talking about it for years to come."

Marsella nodded. “Let’s just hope that your grandfather was telling the truth about the gold. If he wasn’t then this will have all been for nothing.”

Chapter Twenty Five

When Cali came awake he was lying on his back and his head was spinning. The first face he saw was that of a man he didn't recognise. The man was wearing a white gown and had a stethoscope around his neck.

“I’m doctor Lorca,” the man said. “You’re in the hospital in Mestre. You just arrived by water ambulance and I’m pleased to tell you that you are not as seriously injured as was feared.”

The pain behind Cali's brow was abominable. He ran a hand across his scalp and felt a large lump.

“You took a pounding,” the doctor said. “But you were very lucky.”

It came back to Cali then in a rush of graphic images. He could remember the awful sound of the explosion and then the sensation of being lifted off his feet and thrown against something hard.

"What about the others?" he asked.

The doctor's hesitation immediately aroused his suspicion. "What is it, doctor? Tell me."

"The Questore is dead," the doctor said. “I’ve only just been told. He died instantly at the scene apparently. I’m sorry.”

"And the mayor?"

"He’s in much the same condition as yourself. He came across in the same ambulance."

Cali shook his head, which made it hurt even more. It didn't seem possible that Lombardo was dead. He had been with him, and he had been very much alive, such a short time ago.

He felt a ball of emotion well up inside him but he pushed it back down. There was no time for that now. He had to focus on other things.

The doctor helped him to sit up. He rested his back against the plumped-up pillows and tried to gather his thoughts. He was still wearing his clothes and there was dried blood on his shirt front.

"Where was the bomb?" he asked.

"I gather it had been placed in a flower bed up against the wall of your office," the doctor said. "Two more have gone off since then, I'm afraid. One in the docks and another at the municipal police station. One person was killed at the station in Campo Santos and the building suffered extensive damage. It's being evacuated."

Cali felt a pit open up at the bottom of his stomach. For a few seconds his thoughts tossed around in a sea of confusion. Then he sighed, a long, deep sigh that seemed to come from the core of him.

"I've got to get out of here," he said.

"But you're in no fit state. We need to do some x rays to see if there's concussion."

"I'll be all right," Cali said. "Just give me something for the pain."

Cali hauled himself off the bed and was at once hit by a wave of nausea. He held on to the doctor's arm and closed his eyes until the pain and shadows receded.

"You need to rest," the doctor said.

Cali shook his head. "I can't stay here while the city is being systematically destroyed."

"But you..."

Cali dismissed the doctor's objection with a wave of his hand and shuffled into the hallway. There was a Carabinieri officer outside the room, who told him that Salvatore Vitale had ordered him to wait there and report to him when Cali was awake.

"Where is Salvatore now?" Cali asked.

"The Carabinieri station in Mestre," the officer said. "He came across to brief the Prime Minister who arrived a short time ago."

"Then call up a car and take me there."

While he waited outside he phoned his wife to assure her that he was OK. She hadn't even heard that he'd been hurt so she freaked out and it took a while to calm her down.

"I'm fine," he said, and then briefly explained what had happened. Susanna was shocked to hear that Lombardo was dead.

"That's terrible," she said.

"I know and when this is all over we'll grieve for him. But right now there's no time. Where are you?"

"We're on the mainland," she said. "We're staying with Fabio and his wife. I'll come straight to the hospital to be with you."

"There's no point," he said. "I've just discharged myself. I need to get back to work."

"But that's insane. You should stay put."

"There's too much to do. I can't afford to lie around in bed. So just take care of yourself and the boys and I'll call you in a little while. I promise."

She started to respond but he said he had to go and hung up. Just then a police car appeared in front of the hospital.

He climbed in the back and told the driver to take him to the Carabinieri station.

*

The journey would normally have taken five minutes, but because of the crowds that thronged the streets it took nearer thirty. Everywhere Cali looked there were bemused and distraught faces, thousands of them, lining the pavements five deep, packed into coaches, buses, cars and lorries.

The square in front of the Carabinieri station was also packed solid, but a path was made for his vehicle.

Inside the building he was led to the local Commander's office. There was a group of men inside including the Prime Minister, a short, plump man in a smart blue suit. He had grey hair and a dour expression. His eyes were the colour of dark chocolate.

The PM got to his feet and thrust out a hand. "Good to see you, Colonel. I hope you're feeling better."

Cali shook the proffered hand. "Battered and bruised but alive, thank God."

"I heard about the Questore, who I gather was a friend of yours, so may I offer my condolences."

"He was a good man," Cali said.

"So I've been told."

After a long and awkward silence the Prime Minister gestured towards Salvatore and said, "Officer Vitale has explained the situation. I gather the evacuation is going well and is proving less of a problem than we expected."

"That's a relief," Cali said, as he dropped into a chair and wiped the sweat from his forehead.

"I flew down as soon as I could," the PM said. "I felt I had to be here."

"I'm glad you did," Cali said. "At least you can provide some moral support."

Cali turned to Salvatore and said, "So give me an update."

Salvatore explained that most of the city would be clear in a couple of hours.

"We're talking about almost two hundred thousand people."

Cali was surprised that so many people could be moved in such a short time. But then Italy's law enforcement agencies had a vast amount of experience when it came to controlling crowds.

"There's something else you need to know," Salvatore said. "Ten minutes ago I had a call from the morgue, just before the doctor was forced to evacuate."

"Oh?"

“The doctor carried out an emergency autopsy on Enrico Barone and discovered that he did not die of natural causes.”

“Jesus,” Cali said.

“Traces of a digitalis drug were found inside the body. It's a substance that can stimulate and simulate a heart attack. The doctor also found a syringe mark in his neck where the digitalis may have been injected."

"You mean he was poisoned?"

"Seems like it. Obviously by someone who wanted us to think he died naturally”

“But I don’t understand,” the PM said. “Why would anyone do that?”

Cali thought for a moment and said, “To make us think that Barone was working alone. When in truth he had an accomplice.”

“But what would be the point?” the PM said.

Cali shrugged. “It could be they wanted us to believe there was no way of stopping the bombs going off.”

“But that’s absurd.”

“Perhaps not. Let’s consider the facts. We now know that Barone was murdered and that the New Red Brigades are almost certainly behind it. But what we don’t know is what their game plan is. Why kill one of their own and try to make us believe that he died of a heart attack? And why leave the letter for us to find? I’m beginning to wonder if these bombs are being detonated with the sole purpose of making us clear the city.”

“But for what reason?” the PM said.

"That would be the million dollar question," Cali said. "And right now I don't have the answer."

"Could their intention be to loot some of the city's treasures?" Salvatore asked.

Cali shook his head. "I doubt it. They'd surely know we'd take precautions against looters and they'd struggle to get into museums and art galleries following a lock down of the city."

"But if they've deliberately engineered this evacuation then it must be for a reason other than to secure the release of some prisoners," the PM said.

Cali nodded. "Exactly. We should alert our teams to be on the lookout for anything suspicious. Get the navy to patrol the lagoon and the air force to monitor the situation from above. If something is going to happen I suspect it will be during the night when the city is empty and in darkness."

"But what the hell could it be?" the PM said.

Cali looked at him and shrugged. "God only knows, sir."

*

At 10:30pm, Venice was plunged into darkness when the main electricity supply to the city was severed by a huge explosion. Cali and the PM watched it from a first floor window of the Carabinieri station on the mainland.

Cali wondered if it was part of some grand plan, to extinguish the lights so that nobody would be able to see what was going on.

He was still staring out the window when Salvatore came into the office clutching a sheet of paper. "Sir, a message just came in from Milan. They think they have an ID on the man Rienzi saw at the landing stage."

"Read it out," Cali said.

"The description fits one Mario Scalise," Cali said. "He's a leading member of the northern cell of the New Red Brigades and he's also an explosives expert. He was pulled in last year on a conspiracy to murder charge, but managed to get off it after the chief prosecution witness mysteriously disappeared. He usually works under the command of Nicolas Marsella, who is believed to be a key figure in the organisation. The pair of them were last seen together three weeks ago in Rome. Apparently Barone worked with the same group."

"Then it fits," Cali said.

The PM shrugged. "It still doesn't tell us why they've gone to such trouble to empty the city of people."

"Have we a photo of Scalise?" Cali asked.

"It'll be here shortly."

"Have as many copies as possible printed and get them distributed. You'd also better alert the teams to watch out for other known faces including Marsella."

Cali finally received confirmation from the operations room that Venice had been virtually cleared of people. The helicopter pilots were reporting that the streets were empty and the city was almost like a graveyard.

"I don't like it," Cali said. "Something must be in the wind. Otherwise none of this makes sense."

He told Salvatore to pick five of his best men and get a police launch.

"What do you intend to do?" the PM asked.

"Tour the city and look around," Cali said. "Maybe we'll strike lucky and find out what the hell is going on."

"But what about the bombs? There are still dozens of them waiting to explode."

"It's a risk we have to take," Cali said.

Chapter Twenty Six

Marsella looked at his watch. 10:50pm. He turned to Scalise and said, "Take a look at the list. Tell me where the next explosion will be."

Scalise took a notebook from his pocket and consulted it. "The Frari," he said.

Marsella grinned. That would be one in the eye for the establishment. The Santa Maria Gloriosa dei Frari, built in the 14th century by the friars of St Francis, was the most important example of Gothic architecture in Venice and the largest church after St Mark's Basilica. Inside there were priceless works of art, including the Assumption of the Virgin by Titian, which stood proudly behind the main altar.

"It's timed to go off about now," Scalise added.

No sooner had he spoken than the sound of the explosion ripped through the still night like thunder, the blast sending up a flash of orange that illuminated a large part of the city like a bolt of lightning.

"Poor old Titian," Marsella remarked, recalling that the bomb had been planted under the building in a drainage pipe.

A minute later the door opened and a young man hurried into the room. A machine pistol was slung across his back on a strap and on a belt around his waist he carried a holstered revolver, a flashlight, and a two-way radio.

"We've been as far as the Ponte Della Liberta in one direction and San Marco in the other," he said. "The place is like a ghost town. Nothing's moving. It's weird."

"Did the helicopter pilots see you?"

"No. They passed directly overhead at one point, but we ducked out of sight."

"What about the police building?"

"It was cleared out after Cristina detonated the bomb. There's damage to offices at the rear but the reception area remains in one piece. We watched it for a while and there was no sign of life. Cristina has returned there to wait for us."

Marsella grinned. "Did you come across any police patrols or troops?"

"No sign of uniforms on the streets, but there are launches patrolling some of the canals."

Marsella turned to Greco. "Are the guys in position?"

"We're ready to move as soon as you give the word.

Marsella looked again at his watch and said, "The three devices on the causeway are timed to explode in precisely one minute. When they do we go."

The three bombs went off simultaneously. They'd been positioned to cause serious damage to the road linking Venice to the mainland. They would also provide a vital distraction, diverting the attention of the police patrols and chopper pilots away from the city centre.

"That's it," Marsella said. "Let's move."

In the street outside the apartment block the terrorists gathered. There were eight of them and they were all armed to the teeth and dressed in dark jackets and polo sweaters.

Four of them were carrying large black holdalls containing the equipment needed to get to the gold under the floor of the police station.

Marsella addressed the group, saying, "You all know what to do. You two go to the south and east entrances to the square. Patrelli, you go to the bridge to cover the canal approach. When you take up positions report to me by radio using the designated frequency. The rest of you follow me."

They moved through the streets like shadows. The darkness was thick and damp.

Their footfalls echoed loudly in the still night. Normally at this hour the street would have been bustling with people. Many of the cafes would have been open and most of the bars. Tourists would have been everywhere, enjoying an after-dinner stroll or gazing thoughtfully into the lighted windows of the shops.

The terrorists made the only sound as they marched like a small well-disciplined army, their eyes darting from side to side.

They took their time. They needed only a few hours. Then they'd be on their way and nobody would be wise to what they'd done.

It took the group ten minutes to walk to the municipal police building in Campo Santos. The right side of the building had been severely damaged by the bomb Cristina had planted. There was a mound of rubble and the glass was missing from most of the windows.

But the front doors were still intact and suddenly these were pushed open and a figure stepped out. It was Cristina and she had a broad smile on her face.

"It's empty," she called out. "So let's start digging."

Chapter Twenty Seven

Cali stood on the open deck of the police launch as it moved into the Cannaregio canal. He was wearing a police flak jacket over his blood-stained shirt and his face was a mask of trepidation.

The decaying tenements, some six storeys high, rose sheer on either side, no light showing, just ebony walls and water that reflected a pale, vaporous moon.

"It's creepy," someone said and Cali nodded agreement.

The launch made a soft puttering sound as it passed below the first bridge. Half the men were looking to the left, the other half to the right. A searchlight mounted on top of the cabin moved back and forth slowly from one side of the canal to the other. They cruised under a much larger bridge and then, just ahead, the Grand Canal opened out before them.

This was usually one of the busiest intersections on the big canal, being only a few hundred yards from the railway station and Cali had never seen it so still and peaceful.

There were a couple of other police boats and small naval vessels on the canal, heading in both directions, the crews looking out for people who needed help.

Cali had been told that hundreds of residents had probably remained in their homes, ignoring warnings to get out. There wasn't much the authorities could do about them other than to hope that their houses and apartment blocks had not been targeted by the bombers.

Those people were probably thinking that the odds on becoming a victim were still pretty remote given the size of the city. It made Cali think about Lombardo and how he had died. The Questore had been unlucky. He'd been in the wrong place at the wrong time. As Cali thought about it a visceral, raw anger spread through him. He wanted more than anything to hold someone responsible. It wouldn't be Enrico Barone, of course. But it could be those who had been working with him.

*

Inside the three-storey police building the terrorists were hard at work. They had cleared the desks and furniture out of the reception area and four men were pounding away at the tiled floor with pneumatic drills.

The light came from battery-operated lanterns that had been placed around the room and gave off an eerie orange glow.

The terrorists were spread throughout the building at various windows observing the streets. They maintained radio contact with those staking out the approaches to the square.

Greco and Scalise were standing just inside the front entrance, checking and rechecking the two sets of plans that were laid out on a table. The basement access point showed up on the old plans and they were digging in that area.

Greco was a bundle of nerves, not because he was worried they'd be discovered, but because he feared there might not be any gold. After all, he really had only his grandfather's word to go on.

Cristina brought them some coffee from a little kitchen behind the reception desk and Greco smiled his thanks.

Marsella stood to one side watching the drillers. He was looking hot and tense and his forehead was beaded with sweat. He rocked back and forth on his heels, his arms folded across his chest. Every few minutes he checked his watch, growing anxious because the longer they were here the more likely it was they would be discovered.

Suddenly one of the drillers began to shout excitedly for Marsella to come over to where he was working.

"What is it?" Marsella said as he hurried over.

"I've found the hatch," the man said between breaths.

Marsella got down and inspected the area that had been dug up. Sure enough there was the outline of a wooden hatch cover. The concrete around it was ripped up in a matter of minutes. Then the debris was cleared by hand.

It took a while to lift the hatch and when it was open the smell of damp rose up with a vengeance.

Although the basement was wet it wasn't flooded. The steps were still intact after all these years and Marsella went down first followed by Greco.

Their flashlights immediately revealed a number of crates stacked floor to ceiling and the two men squealed with delight.

With trembling hands they wasted no time forcing open one of the crates and sure enough they found it to be full of shiny gold ingots.

Chapter Twenty Eight

Cali directed the police launch along the entire length of the Grand Canal. It was a surreal experience for all the officers on board.

Palls of grey smoke hung above the city and the air was filled with the acrid smell of burning.

There was no conversation. The team remained silent as they stared at the silhouettes of the Renaissance palaces on either side of the canal. Here and there a light shone or flickered beyond a window and shapes moved in the darkness.

The life had been sucked out of Venice in a matter of hours and now the city was in a state of paralysis. Cali wondered if it would ever recover and not just from the physical damage to the ancient infrastructure. The very heart of Venice had been punctured by this callous act of terrorism.

He didn't doubt that many of those who had been evacuated to the mainland would never return. They would join the thousands who had already left the city in recent years. The shrinking population had for so long been a big concern and now it would become an even more calamitous issue.

There was suddenly more activity up ahead where navy vessels and police boats gathered in St Mark's basin, the water space in front of the piazza.

They were positioned between the city and the outlying islands and their brief was to ensure that private craft did not flee the area with looted treasure on board.

Protecting the city's priceless antiquities from bombs and looters was not an easy task in the circumstances. There was only so much that could be done when the priority was to ensure that as many people as possible were moved out of harm's way.

Cali got the pilot to turn the launch into one of the smaller canals and at once the atmosphere became ominously claustrophobic. The buildings on either side pressed in on them, but nothing they saw from the boat gave rise to suspicion. The streets were empty, the silence deafening.

But in an instant things changed.

It happened unexpectedly when they turned a corner and the searchlight swept across the canal and onto a small bridge about thirty yards ahead.

A man on top of the bridge was caught in the glare. His upper body was visible above the parapet and Cali and the others saw him clearly.

Cali instinctively wondered what he was doing there. But he became instantly more curious when the man suddenly ducked down out of sight.

His reaction surprised all those on board who saw it and an officer grabbed a megaphone and called out to him.

"We are the Carabinieri. Please identify yourself."

But the man on the bridge did not respond and Cali's senses immediately kicked into overdrive. He experienced a flutter of unease as he withdrew his revolver from its holster.

The bridge was now only about fifteen yards ahead and the launch was going to pass beneath it. There was no way of knowing if the man was still up there. Or why he saw fit to hide. It made Cali feel distinctly uncomfortable.

Something wasn't right. He knew it, but he had no time to react. As they approached the bridge he stared up to where the searchlight's beam splashed against the ancient brickwork.

And that's when the man suddenly appeared again. Only this time he was brandishing an automatic weapon.

*

The gun exploded and a hail of shells rained down on the launch, striking bodies and slamming into the open parts of the deck.

The four officers at the front of the launch – including the pilot – were targeted first. Cali, who was standing on the rear deck with one other officer, watched as the men were mercilessly cut down. They stood no chance as round after round tore into them, puffing up blood and gore.

Before Cali could even get off a single shot he was forced to crouch down behind the low-slung cabin between the two open decks. But the officer next to him was slower to react and took three bullets in quick succession, one to the face and two to the chest.

Cali braced himself, knowing that he was about to be exposed as the launch moved under the bridge, giving the gunman a clear view of him.

But he wasn't going to make it easy for the bastard. With nothing to lose he sprang up and fired indiscriminately in his direction.

He was convinced he'd be hit and squeezed his eyes shut in anticipation. He felt a bullet whistle past his left ear and another slammed into the roof of the cabin just inches from his chest.

But then the launch puttered under the bridge and the exchange of fire halted.

Cali opened his eyes, astonished that he was still alive, and mindful of the fact that in about two seconds he wouldn't be when the launch emerged on the other side.

The boat was still going at about five knots and there'd be no stopping it until it crashed.

Cali knew his only chance was to get into the canal, so he immediately threw himself over the side. The water was black and freezing and as he went under he reached out blindly and somehow managed to get a grip on the underside of the footplate at the stern of the boat.

As he was pulled forward through the dark water he heaved his legs up beneath the hull in a desperate bid to shield his body from the killer on the bridge.

He made it just in time.

The gunfire started up again and the shells zinged into the water all around him.

He pressed himself against the hull and clung on for his life. The launch kept going in a straight line and the sound of the gunfire was drowned out by the roar of the engine.

Cali held his breath and tried to ignore the fire in his lungs. His head was being buffeted by the churning water and he could feel his fingers slipping.

Eventually he had to let go of the footplate and push his head out of the water. Gasping for breath, he forced his eyes open and watched the boat moving away. He saw also that there was a bend up ahead so with no pilot at the wheel it was sure to crash.

Treading water, Cali twisted his body and looked back towards the bridge. To his immense relief there was no sign of the gunman, although in the dark it was difficult to be sure.

But it didn't mean he was out of the danger zone. The gunman was probably racing to a point further along the canal where he could intercept the boat.

There were buildings on either side of him, mostly old warehouses and decaying tenements. Just above the water line were a series of arched doorways, some of them with iron bars to stop people getting in.

His options were limited. He could go back towards the bridge or try to get into one of the buildings. The latter seemed to be the most sensible option so he struck out towards the side of the canal. As he did so he heard an almighty *thud* as the police boat crashed into a building.

He ignored the temptation to look and kept going until he reached one of the thick wooden poles that reared up out of the water. He held onto it while he fought to regain his breath and search the darkness.

He heard shouting and feared he was about to have a light shone on him. But thankfully it didn't happen and after a moment he moved away from the wooden pole and pulled himself along the side of the canal by grabbing rusting pipes, damaged bricks and slabs of concrete that jutted out.

After about a minute he got lucky when he saw that one of the arched doorways had no door or bars. With breathless determination he pulled himself up onto a raised ledge and stepped, shivering, into the pitch-black interior.

The smell hit him like a hard slap, a putrid mix of damp and mould and rotten animal flesh. He stood for a moment so his eyes could adjust to the darkness.

He'd been in buildings like this countless times. There were hundreds of them throughout Venice and they lined many of the canals. At some point in the past they had been proud and perhaps palatial, but having been abandoned they were now just grim shells that were home to colonies of rodents.

This particular building looked to Cali as though it had last been used as a warehouse and he was standing in what was once the loading area. Despite the gloom he could make out the high, beamed ceiling and the large area of floor space. There were some damaged wooden crates over to his left and the concrete floor was littered with all kinds of debris.

He shoved his hand in his jacket pocket to see if he still had his phone. He did, but the water had rendered it useless. He quickly removed the battery and blew it dry. Then he tried again but still it refused to work.

Damn.

He took a deep breath and started walking across the room. His legs felt heavy and weak and his body began to shake with the cold.

But he was determined to ignore his discomfort and focus his mind on what he had to do: *which was to get out of there and raise the alarm.*

The gunman on the bridge must have had a reason for opening fire on the launch. Its sudden appearance had seemingly panicked him - but why?

He needed to find out what the guy had been doing on the bridge. Did it have something to do with the bombs? Was he involved with the men whose names he had been given earlier - Nicolas Marsella and Mario Scalise? And if so what was their game?

The questions swirled around inside his head as he made his way across the room, as much by touch as by sight.

He came to a flight of stairs and climbed them holding on to a loose banister. At the top of the stairs it got even darker and he had to feel his way along a narrow corridor with an uneven floor. The damp walls seemed to amplify his rapid breathing.

There were several boarded up windows on his right and further on he came to a large door that looked as though it hadn't been opened in years.

But the timber appeared weathered and weak and Cali reckoned he'd be able to kick it open from the inside.

But before he attempted to do so he stood with his ear to the door listening for sounds outside. All he could hear was the distant hum of a helicopter. No shouts or footfalls.

The first two kicks did nothing more than cause the door to splinter above and below the rusty hinges. But the third kick did the trick and the door flew open.

As Cali stepped outside onto a cobbled street he inhaled deeply on the fresh, crisp air and felt the relief surge through him.

But as he turned to look along the street he saw a dark figure step into view about twenty yards away.

A nanosecond later came a blast of gunfire.

Chapter Twenty Nine

The sound of more gunfire troubled Marsella. He took it to mean that his man was struggling to cope with the threat from the Carabinieri.

When Patrelli had radioed from the bridge to tell him that a police launch was heading towards their location he had given the order to kill everyone on board before they could raise the alarm.

The sound of Patrelli's Uzi exploding was heard seconds later and Marsella had assumed the job was done and the Carabinieri would not suddenly appear on the scene to scupper the operation.

But now this latest spurt of gunfire. The last thing he needed was for the cops to arrive before the crates of gold had been taken to the warehouse. And that was still at least thirty minutes away.

Six crates had so far been extracted from the basement below the reception area and were piled up outside ready to be carried the two hundred yards or so to the old warehouse. Everything had gone to plan until now and Marsella had started to believe that they would pull it off without a single hitch.

But the sudden arrival of the paramilitary police was a salutary reminder that they still had some way to go. And every step of the way was fraught with danger and risk.

He summoned Cristina and Scalise and told them to go to the bridge which was only a few streets away.

"The cops might have called for reinforcements," he said. "If so then do whatever it takes to keep them away from here for as long as you can. We need time to get the gold to the warehouse."

Scalise and Cristina responded immediately, like trained soldiers obeying an order from a superior officer. They hurried off in the direction of the bridge, armed with their Uzis and a rigid determination to ensure that the operation was a success.

As Marsella watched them disappear into the dark he felt confident that his two most trusted operatives would not let him down.

Even if it meant sacrificing their own lives in the process.

Chapter Thirty

Cali was still alive.

Just.

Somehow he'd managed to duck into the alley opposite the warehouse as the volley of shots rang out. At least one shell slammed into the wall only inches from his head. Another smashed a window behind him.

He ran with his head down, forcing his limbs into an uneven rhythm.

The alleyway was short and dark and the only exit was at the far end. He had to cover maybe thirty yards and he wasn't sure he'd make it before the gunman reached the alley and had him in his sights again.

Cali's wet shoes pounded away on the paving stones and his heart pounded in his chest.

There was just enough light from the moon to see the ground but his vision was blurred and his head was spinning wildly. He knew that if he encountered an obstacle in the alley he probably wouldn't see it.

He really did not expect to make it to the end of the alley. As he hurled himself towards the junction there came another blast of gunfire. He was lucky, though. The shooter was firing blind whilst on the move so he couldn't find his target.

Thank God.

Cali reached the end of the alley and veered to the left, putting the corner of the building between himself and his pursuer. But he came to an abrupt halt when he realised that the street he was on offered no cover ahead. On his right was a canal, its water black and still, and on his left buildings with doorways flush against the wall.

He decided there was only one way out of this, so he swung round and stood firm, his legs apart, his fists clenched. He blew out a hard breath and waited.

Five seconds later a dark, silhouetted figure emerged from the alley at full pelt. Cali pounced on him without warning.

He threw himself into the man like a hard-headed rugby player. The guy was taken by surprise. He let out a loud grunt and staggered backwards, dropping his weapon.

They both went crashing to the ground. Their foreheads came together with a loud, agonizing crack that had Cali reeling with pain.

But he managed not to lose control and quickly seized the man's throat, digging his fingers into the soft flesh.

As the man started to writhe and panic, Cali got a sense of his size and stature. He was strong and lean with broad shoulders and a hard body beneath a black leather jacket.

The man shook himself free of Cali's grip and for about half a minute the pair were locked in a vicious struggle. Cali's age and level of fitness put him at a disadvantage, but the raw hatred he felt for this man who had shot his five colleagues gave him strength. He was salivating with anger as he punched, kicked and clawed at his opponent.

But the man was no slouch. He fought back ferociously and thrashed around with enough force to push Cali away from him. The man then rolled over and scrambled for his weapon. He managed to grab it by the barrel and pull it towards him across the concrete.

But Cali was quick to recover. He sprang at the man and struck him full in the face with a sold punch.

The man cried out and let go of the gun. At the same time Cali grabbed a handful of his hair and yanked his head off the ground before slamming it back down on the cold concrete.

There was a loud crack of bone and the guy issued a painful grunt.

Cali tried to repeat the action but the man seized his wrist with both hands. Cali countered by letting go of the man's hair and as the head fell back he jammed his fingers into the man's right eye.

The man let go of Cali's wrist and Cali took the opportunity to heave himself up onto his knees. He picked up the guy's weapon and smashed the butt end against the man's forehead.

Once.

Twice.

Three times.

He was so enraged, crimson clouded his vision.

With each blow came the sound of bone shattering and flesh being ripped open. It was too dark to see the full extent of the damage he'd inflicted, but he could tell that the gunman's face had been reduced to a bloody mess. If he wasn't already dead then he soon would be. But Cali didn't care. The murdering bastard deserved to die.

He got up and then gagged, spat and sucked in great chunks of air. He felt bruised and weak, but he was grateful, and surprised, that he was still alive.

There was no time to reflect on his good fortune, though. His mind was racing and he needed to find out what was going on.

Why had this man opened fire on the police launch?

Why had he tried to make sure there were no survivors?

As Cali stood there his breath came back in tight bursts and the adrenaline surged through him like water through a fire hose.

When he had his breathing under control he knelt down and searched the gunman. His pockets were empty except for a flashlight. There was no wallet or ID and no phone.

Cali switched on the flashlight and shone it on the man's face. The sight of it gave him a jolt. Two things were startlingly obvious. The man was dead. And even his own mother wouldn't recognise him.

Cali forced down a wave of nausea and got to his feet. He switched off the flashlight and put it in his pocket. Then he picked up the weapon – which he now realised was an Uzi sub-machine gun.

But as he started to move away a garbled voice from on the ground made him stop. He froze and stared down at the gunman. Impossible, he told himself. The guy was dead or dying and no way should he be talking.

Cali whipped the flashlight from his pocket and turned it on. And in an instant he realised that the voice was coming from a small two-way radio. He hadn't spotted it when searching the man's pockets because it was attached to his belt at the back and hidden from view.

Cali reached down and unclipped it. Just as he did so the voice came through again, barely audible through the rumble of abrasive static.

"Come in, Patrelli. What the hell is going on there? If you're in trouble then hold firm. I'm sending help."

Chapter Thirty One

So the dead man was part of a team. And they were communicating with each other by radio.

The revelation came not so much as a shock to Cali as confirmation that his suspicions had been justified. He had ventured into the deserted city to find out if something sinister was going down. And he had stumbled on to the devastating truth.

Whatever was in play involved men with automatic weapons, men who were now desperate to stop him from raising the alarm and bringing in the troops.

It was logical to conclude that what was happening here was connected with the explosions. And it was clear to him now that their aim was not to secure the release of New Red Brigades prisoners. There was another reason.

But what the hell were they up to? Why go to such extraordinary lengths to force the authorities to clear Venice of people?

The questions were piling up inside his head, making it difficult for him to focus on what he needed to do. It felt like his skull was on fire.

He stared at the radio in his hand and for a moment thought of responding to whoever was on the other end. But he decided against it and shoved it into his pocket along with the flashlight.

Then, armed with the Uzi, he started back towards the alley. In the distance he could hear the beat of a helicopter's rotor blades, but other than that the city remained silent.

He moved quickly, but cautiously, his finger heavy on the trigger, his heart tattooing in his chest.

He could see the warehouse up ahead, on the street where the gunman had spotted him. Close by was the canal and the police launch. He remembered spotting a couple of shops and offices and one or more of them was bound to contain a phone. But he knew he would have to be careful. If he made a lot of noise he would draw attention to himself and God only knew how many other terrorists would descend on him.

As he walked he felt fear flow through him in a cold ripple. He had never in his entire life been so scared. Not just for him, but for the city and its people.

When he reached the other end of the alley he stopped to peer out into the cobbled street. It was empty. He turned right and moved slowly forward, his finger poised nervously on the Uzi's trigger.

He walked passed two small shops and an office entrance. All the doors and windows were closed and locked and he was reluctant to force them open for fear of revealing his position. It was frustrating, but until he knew where the other terrorists were he was determined to play safe.

He followed the street for another twenty yards and came to another junction. He was about to turn the corner when he heard a voice. It was close by and he was pretty sure it belonged to a woman.

He clenched his jaw and tightened his grip on the Uzi.

The voice was growing louder, coming closer. Shit. The woman was walking towards him.

He could not make out what she was saying but he was certain it was a one-way conversation. It sounded like she was talking into a radio.

As he listened his stomach twisted in grim apprehension and he made up his mind to surprise her before she stepped into view and maybe got the drop on him.

He held his breath until he reckoned she was only a few feet away.

Then he leapt out in front of her.

Chapter Thirty Two

The woman was caught unawares and gave a high-pitched yelp as Cali suddenly confronted her.

She was by herself and before she could respond he lashed out with the Uzi and smashed it against her chest. He used enough force to knock her to the ground. Then he followed through with a wild kick that struck her weapon and sent it spinning out of her hands.

As she tried to get up he stamped on her chest and pressed the muzzle of the Uzi against her throat.

"Be still or I'll kill you," he warned her.

She let out a pitiful gasp and lay there on her back as Cali used his free hand to take out the flashlight and shine it on her face.

He judged her to be in her late twenties. Her dark, lustrous hair was tied back into a ponytail and her face was thin and pale and not unattractive. She too was wearing a leather jacket and beneath it a black polo sweater.

"Who are you?" he said.

She gritted her teeth and her wide eyes went narrow with rage.

"I'm a citizen of Venice," she yelled back at him. "Why are you doing this to me?"

He put pressure on the Uzi until she whimpered in pain.

"You're a terrorist," he said. "Your accomplice slaughtered my colleagues on the Carabinieri launch and you were sent here to find and kill me."

She shook her head. "You're crazy. I don't know what you're talking about."

"You're a liar. Citizens of Venice don't walk around with machine guns. Now tell me who you are and what you're doing here."

"I've given you my answer," she said. "Now I demand that you let me go."

The woman drilled him with a hard stare and he felt sorely tempted to pull the trigger.

"Where are the rest of your team?" he pressed her.

"Go to hell," she spat at him.

The rage was tearing through him now and he was struggling to control it. The bitch was playing for time and he couldn't let her get away with it.

He straightened his arm and moved the Uzi so the muzzle was pressed firmly against her forehead.

"I'm going to give you five seconds to tell me what I want to know," he said. "If you don't I swear I'll shoot you."

As he counted backwards out loud the woman remained tight-lipped and defiant. Her eyes glittered fiercely and she pinched her face into a mocking smile.

Cali's heart was pumping blood so fast it was making him feel dizzy. Cords of saliva foamed at the corners of his mouth.

"Three…two…"

He felt the heat of tears rise behind his eyes as he prepared to fire the Uzi.

But just as his resolve was about to be tested he heard a sudden rush of footfalls on the cobbles behind him.

*

Cali spun round and saw a man bearing down on him.

In the millisecond before he could react his brain registered two alarming facts: The man was no more than fifteen yards away, and he was taking aim with a weapon.

Cali instinctively dodged to one side, dropping the flashlight as he squeezed the Uzi's trigger. There was a bright muzzle flash as the gun jumped in his hand and a rapid burst of fire sent a spray of shells in every direction.

The Uzi kicked back with such ferocity it caused him to stumble. He let out a wordless cry and heard shells punch into the wall above him.

The shattering noise of the gunfire imploded in his skull, but he kept squeezing the trigger and waving the weapon.

Crack! Crack! Crack!

His right shoulder slammed against a wall and the impact forced out a guttural moan. But he somehow managed to stay on his feet and when he heard his assailant shriek in pain he guessed that at least one bullet had struck home.

At the same time an amorphous shape moved quickly in his peripheral vision. It was the woman, clambering up from the ground. Cali twisted his body round and stretched out his arm.

Crack!

A single blast and he saw her fall to the ground. He'd aimed low in the hope of hitting a leg but he couldn't be sure where the bullet struck because of the monumental noise and confusion.

His vision clouded momentarily as his senses fought to stay focused. Everything seemed to be happening with a curious dreamlike slowness.

Then a new sound caught his attention and drew his eyes skywards. It was the unmistakable roar of a helicopter that suddenly appeared overhead, its searchlight sweeping the city in a wide arc.

Much to Cali's dismay it did not hover directly above. Instead it soared across the narrow gap between the buildings and out of sight.

But he was reassured by its pulsing presence and hoped it meant that his people were now aware of all the commotion and had come to investigate. Maybe they had even spotted the Carabinieri launch.

He shook his head to clear his vision and took up a defensive position with his back to the wall.

But in the sudden silence he saw that he was no longer under attack. To his left lay the man who had tried to kill him. He was splayed on his back and there was a delicate frond of blood on the ground next to his head.

In the gloom Cali could just about make out his pale features but he wasn't close enough to be certain that he was dead. He wasn't moving, though, so Cali did not perceive him to be an immediate threat.

He turned towards where the woman had fallen and was shocked to see that she was no longer there. Cautiously, he stepped away from the wall and looked both ways along the street. There was no sign of her. But he did spot a significant amount of blood just beyond where she had fallen.

It told him she'd been wounded and in the chaos had managed to slip away.

Shit.

He pulled a quick breath, pressed his mouth into a thin line and hurriedly followed the trail of blood.

Chapter Thirty Three

Marsella was standing on the steps of the police station when he heard the helicopter approach.

It drowned out the sounds of gunfire and sent a chill along his spine.

He quickly ordered his men to take cover and stepped back through the doorway.

The chopper appeared from over the rooftops, dragging with it a cone of light. He wasn't entirely surprised to see it given all the shooting.

But its arrival caused a red hot rage to burn inside him because he knew it could spell disaster for the operation. All twenty crates of gold had been removed from under the floor of the station, but they were still outside the building waiting to be shifted to the warehouse. Once there they would be safely hidden until such time as they could be transported to the mainland. At least that was the plan.

For an agonising few seconds the chopper hovered above the little square in front of the station, creating a wave of shuddering air beneath its blades.

Marsella watched from just inside the doorway and to his great relief the searchlight did not pass over the crates.

Then his steely eyes glinted with a remote, mirthless grin as the big bird moved slowly away.

He stepped back outside and his gaze swung around the square, which thankfully was still empty.

"OK, let's get these crates to the warehouse," he shouted to his men as they started to emerge from the shadows. "We're running out of time."

He then turned to Greco and said, "I'll help move the stuff. You wait here for Cristina and Scalise. I'm getting worried because they're not answering their radios."

"What about the bomb?" Greco asked, referring to the device they had left inside the police station to help cover their tracks. It was actually the last device they had planted. Barone's note had only been true up to a point. They had assumed the authorities would be forced to clear the city long before midnight so any more devices would not been needed.

But the authorities would spend days, maybe weeks, searching for many more bombs that did not exist.

"As soon as we're clear of here I'll set the timer," Marsella said.

He hurried down the steps and was about to help load the crates onto a small four-wheeled cart that one of the men had brought from the warehouse. But just then there was another blast of sound as the chopper returned. Its dark body appeared suddenly and was much lower in the sky; so low in fact that the ground seemed to shake along with the buildings.

Marsella cursed out loud and experienced a needle-sharp sense of foreboding. He watched the cone of light as it trailed into the square from one of the side streets.

And then he saw something that made his heart stop.

It was Cristina.

She was engulfed by the light as she staggered across the square towards them.

Even from a distance of about twenty yards Marsella could see that she was hurt.

And covered in blood.

Chapter Thirty Four

Cali might have lost the wounded woman if it hadn't been for the helicopter. In the dark it was hard to follow the trail of blood on the ground.

But the roar of the rotor blades was impossible to miss. He heard it before he saw it and headed in that direction.

As he jogged through the narrow streets he still wasn't sure where exactly in the city he was. He was disoriented and traumatised, his breathing laboured from fear and effort. The total lack of lighting made the city unfamiliar. The moon's feeble glow was not in itself sufficient to make the buildings recognisable.

But then he turned a corner and stumbled into the little square. It was starkly illuminated by the helicopter's searchlight. And he knew instantly that it was the Campo Santos. Usually it was quiet and peaceful. Off-duty cops from the municipal police station often sat drinking coffee at the only café facing onto the square.

But that peace was now being shattered and as Cali came to a grinding halt he stared with incredulity at the scene.

It was like the set of a big-budget action movie.

The helicopter was hovering above the square, its downdraught kicking up a storm. The searchlight fell on the woman as she staggered towards the police station building, her body bent double.

Cali rushed into the square waving his arms frantically above his head to attract the attention of the helicopter crew.

"Over here," he yelled. "Carabinieri."

As he closed in on the woman she suddenly collapsed onto the ground, unable to go any further.

Cali got to within a few feet of her before he spotted figures detaching themselves from the shadows of the police station. He saw at least three men. All dressed in black and carrying weapons.

He stopped dead in his tracks and a shudder passed through his body. He wasn't sure what was happening and he instinctively snapped a glance up at the helicopter.

But at the same time shots rang out and he was knocked off his feet by something that exploded against his shoulder.

Chapter Thirty Five

Marsella's first shot struck the man who was chasing Cristina, no doubt a Carabinieri officer from the launch.

As the man's body hit the ground Marsella swung his arm upwards and opened fire on the chopper. Behind him what was left of his team joined in the attack, their aim being to bring the big bird down.

No one needed to be told to target the cockpit and the tail rotor, the most vulnerable parts of the delicately balanced machine. But the first thing to be disabled was the searchlight, plunging the square into darkness.

It meant they couldn't see the pilot struggling to control the beast and within seconds it was in a violent spin.

The chopper was an easy target because the pilot, unaware of the danger from terrorists, had ventured close to the ground. As it plummeted downwards its blades clipped the side of a building, tearing off great blocks of concrete and causing it to flip sideways.

In the split second before it crashed into the square Marsella saw the word CARABINIERI stencilled in large white letters on the dark blue fuselage.

The words disappeared along with the rest of the doomed chopper as it got swallowed up by a huge fireball.

He could feel the scorching heat on his face even though the inferno was on the far side of the square, a safe distance from the crates of gold.

As the helicopter burned furiously Marsella summoned his men together. There were five of them now, including himself. Patrelli and Scalise were missing and Cristina was no longer able to pull her weight.

He wished now he'd brought more people, but during the planning stage they had decided on a small team, believing there was less chance of being seen in a deserted Venice.

He had to shout to make himself heard above the roar of the flames from across the square.

"There's still time to get the gold to the warehouse," he told them. "But police reinforcements are likely to arrive in minutes so we have to move fast. And we can't afford to leave any of the crates behind. If we do it will lead to an extensive search of every building in the area. So get started."

Instead of following his men Marsella turned abruptly and walked over to where Cristina lay on the ground. He knelt beside her and saw in the light from the fire that she was unconscious but still breathing. The front of her sweater was drenched in blood and it looked as though she had been shot in the stomach.

His sympathy for her was tempered by the fact that she had led the Carabinieri to the square. But then she probably hadn't realised it.

He sucked in a long breath through clenched teeth and lifted her up in his arms.

"What the hell are you doing?" came a voice from behind him.

He turned and found himself face to face with Greco.

"Cristina's alive," Marsella said. "I'm taking her with us."

"Don't be a fool. She'll slow us down. We have to leave her."

Marsella shook his head. "No way. She's one of us. And if she survives she might lead the cops to the gold."

"Then we kill her," Greco said.

Marsella's mouth curled into a grimace, ugly and threatening.

"You just do your fucking job and leave the decisions to me," he screamed.

Greco opened his mouth to speak but his eyes shifted suddenly and his face registered alarm.

Marsella followed his stricken gaze and saw that the Carabinieri officer who had fallen just a few yards away was hauling himself up onto his knees.

The flash of the gun in his hand was like a strobe light and Marsella watched, helpless, as Greco's chest was ripped open by a spray of bullets.

Chapter Thirty Six

The pain in Cali's shoulder was excruciating and it took all his strength to heave himself up and let loose with the Uzi.

He'd been lucky. If the bullet fired at him had struck just a couple of inches to the right he'd be dead. As it was he hadn't been rendered unconscious despite losing blood and having to fight against the pitted blackness that was enveloping his vision.

So he heard the helicopter crash and then he heard the terrorists talking among themselves about gold and crates and warehouses. And he knew he had to do something to stop them getting away. Playing dead was not an option.

He was bang on target with his first shot and the man was driven backwards as the bullet smashed into his chest.

Cali then aimed the Uzi at the other man, who quickly dropped the woman's legs and held her body close against him as a shield.

Cali hesitated for just a fraction of a second, but it was time enough for the other terrorists to realise what was happening and open fire.

Cali was forced to throw himself flat on the ground and he heard bullets strike the paving around him.

But he held onto the gun and fired back. There was a deafening barrage of shots. Then suddenly the Uzi stopped kicking back and Cali knew he had run out of ammo.

His pain-racked body was flooded by a sensation of dread. Fearing the worst, he raised his head and took in the scene in front of him.

He saw the woman lying not twelve feet away and next to her the man who had used her as a shield. Then beyond them he saw two men walking towards him through clouds of smoke.

A feeling of nausea rose up through the waves of pain. He knew he was about to die and an image of his wife and sons flashed in his mind. Tears stung his eyes and he let out an involuntary cry.

The two men were dressed in black and carrying automatic weapons. They approached warily and then one of them lowered himself to a squat to check the bodies of their colleagues.

Cali closed his eyes and waited for the end. He wondered if he would hear the shots before the bullets hit him.

But instead he heard something else. It was the familiar rumble of a helicopter fast approaching.

He opened his eyes and saw the two men looking up at the sky. Then they looked briefly at each other and decided it was time to hot-foot it away from there.

As Cali watched them take flight he felt the pain across his chest ease and something close to a smile touched his lips.

*

The helicopter was hovering above the square in a matter of seconds.

Cali managed to get to his feet and wave even though he could feel his strength ebbing away. He wasn't sure if those on board spotted him, but he was confident the square would soon be swarming with cops and paramedics.

As he staggered over to where the woman lay it felt like a strong current was fighting against him. At the same time he started choking on the acrid smell of cordite.

He lowered himself beside the woman and saw immediately that she was dead. A bullet had torn away part of her skull and he felt a spasm of guilt because he knew it had come from his weapon.

He moved on to the guy who had shot him, the one who had spoken as though he was the leader of the group. Much to Cali's surprise he was still alive, but barely. His eyes were open and his face was screwed up in agony. He started to splutter and gasp for breath.

Cali leaned over him and his own blood dripped from his shoulder wound onto the man's jacket.

The man squinted up at him and it occurred to Cali that they might both die together before help arrived.

The man had a chest wound and it was oozing blood. But he wasn't so far gone that he couldn't see Cali. His lips parted slightly and he grunted out a single word.

"Cristina?"

Cali knew he was referring to the woman. He'd heard the name mentioned when the terrorists were talking.

"She's dead," he told him.

The man squeezed his eyes shut and his mouth made a quivering line.

"Who are you?" Cali yelled. "What was all this about?"

The man did not respond so Cali grabbed him by the shoulders and shook him.

"The bombs," he shouted. "Where are the rest of them? Tell me."

But the man's eyes remained closed and the veins in his neck started pumping like pistons.

Cali shook him again but the effort drained him and he became dizzy and nauseous. He felt a heavy weakness consume him, a dull weariness that went beyond exhaustion.

His body gave way then and he keeled over, landing with a painful thud on his injured shoulder.

He clenched his eyes shut and a cold darkness swept over him.

Chapter Thirty Seven

It was a long night and Venice survived it. No more bombs exploded and no more people died. The sun rose early and hung like an over-ripe orange above the city.

Cali woke up in hospital at three in the afternoon. He was attached to various machines including a saline drip and a heart monitor. His shoulder ached beneath padded dressing and he was told that the bullet had been removed and there was no serious internal damage.

Susanna and the boys were there when he came to and he had never been so glad to see them. His wife's eyes were sunken and shadowed and even his sons could not hold back the tears.

He could remember with startling clarity what had happened in the square and he found it hard to accept that he was alive. The images were terrifyingly vivid and flickered through his head in a bizarre slide show.

He was bursting with questions and they were answered gradually throughout the rest of the day by those who came to see him. There was Salvatore and the mayor and even the Prime Minister dropped in to praise him for what he had done.

He was told that the man who had shot him – the terrorist Nicolas Marsella – had survived and was being treated at another hospital. His condition was stable and he would recover to stand trial.

The woman found dead in the square had been identified as Cristina Rebaldo and the other man as Vittore Greco, both known terrorists.

One of the men who had run away from the square had been caught and arrested. The search for others was still going on. The arrested man had in the last couple of hours started talking and had revealed why the New Red Brigades had wanted to clear Venice of people.

Cali listened in stunned disbelief to the story of the gold and how it had been concealed under the floor of the municipal police station for all these years. Rumours that a stash of Nazi treasure had been hidden in Venice towards the end of the war were well known, but nobody had really taken them seriously.

The terrorists' plan was diabolical, but it they had pulled it off the rewards would have been enormous.

According to the guy under arrest only one live bomb remained in the city and that was in the police station itself. The bomb squad were in the process of making it safe.

Discussions were already underway as to how and when people would be allowed back into the city. The authorities wanted to ensure that it was safe first so the military and the various police departments had entered in force to search every building.

The grim tally of those who'd been killed had reached thirty nine, including his good friend the Questore, the Carabinieri officers on the launch with Cali, the two men who crewed the stricken helicopter and three of the terrorists.

He found it hard to take it all in and what he heard put a cold weight in his stomach. But at least it was over and his beloved city had survived yet again.

The damage would be repaired and the dead would be remembered.

And the pigeons would no doubt return to St Mark's Square.

Epilogue

Six months later

In any other city in the world it would have been considered a calamity. But the Venetians took this latest flood in their stride even though the water level peaked at an astonishing 62 inches.

Locals and tourists were forced to don waders and use raised platforms to get around. The heavy rain and high tides had subsided but it would be some time before the streets were dry again.

St Mark's Square was like a huge lake and several hardy souls had even put on swimming costumes to pose for photographs.

It was another reminder of the fragility of this great city. But it was also a testament to the resilience of its people.

True, hundreds more had moved to the mainland since the terrorist bombings, but in every other sense life in the city was back to normal.

Bells rang and gondoliers plied their trade along the Grand Canal. Artists gathered in the palazzos and an endless flotilla of speedboats and water buses moved people and goods around the city.

The damage caused by the terrorists was being repaired and the buildings that had been targeted would soon be gloriously impressive once again.

Venice was back in business and everyone agreed it would remain one of the world's top tourist attractions.

At least until it finally sank without trace beneath the cool waters of the Adriatic.

The End

http://www.james-raven.com/

Also by James Raven

Rollover
Urban Myth
Arctic Blood
Stark Warning
Brutal Revenge
After the Execution

Printed in Great Britain
by Amazon